Frank Samuel Child

An Old New England Town

Sketches of Life, Scenery, Character. Second Edition

Frank Samuel Child

An Old New England Town
Sketches of Life, Scenery, Character. Second Edition

ISBN/EAN: 9783337013585

Printed in Europe, USA, Canada, Australia, Japan

Cover: Foto ©Andreas Hilbeck / pixelio.de

More available books at **www.hansebooks.com**

AN OLD NEW ENGLAND TOWN

EDITION DE LUXE in octavo, limited to twenty-five copies, printed throughout on Japan paper, numbered 1 to 25. *Not for sale.*

Two hundred and seventy-five copies printed on special paper, illustrations on Japan paper, numbered 26 to 300. *Net $5.00*

REGULAR EDITION in 12mo. *Net $2.00*

Indices Reaes. H. Sherman.

An Old
New England Town

SKETCHES OF
LIFE, SCENERY, CHARACTER

BY

Frank Samuel Child

With Illustrations

SECOND EDITION

NEW YORK
CHARLES SCRIBNER'S SONS
1895

To
The Eunice Dennie Burr Chapter
of
The Daughters of the American Revolution
Perpetuating the
Old-Time and the New-Time
Spirit of Patriotism

PREFACE.

THE old New England town has peculiar interest for us. It has taken a conspicuous part in the development of our social life and political institutions. And there are few towns that have achieved a more honorable distinction than Fairfield.

Mindful of this fact, the Daughters of the American Revolution who constitute the Eunice Dennie Burr Chapter invited the writer of the following papers to give a course of lectures upon the old New England town which was especially dear to them. He was pleased to accept this courteous invitation, for his love of Fairfield was deep and strong, and he appreciated the fact that the town had made large and notable contributions to the life of the Colony and the Republic.

Arrangements for the lectures were consummated ; members of the Dorothy Ripley Chapter, of Southport, members of the Mary Silliman Chapter, of Bridgeport, and other friends interested in local history were invited to be present. The large audiences in attendance, and the close attention paid, evidenced the importance of the events, individuals, matters discussed.

At the conclusion of the lectures it was the wish of many people that the papers should be given to the public in book form. It was also suggested that illustrations would add to the value and pleasure of the book. The writer takes this opportunity of expressing thanks to the kind and generous friends that have aided him in these tasks.

In respect to the subject-matter of the book, it is to be distinctly understood that the author has not attempted to write a history. He has gleaned from public and private sources, from official documents and family treasures, the numerous facts and incidents related. But the purpose has been simply to etch a series of pictures so that the life of former days might come before the hearer or the reader with a fair degree of accuracy and suggestiveness. The author has had every privilege and opportunity granted him by numerous private individuals of Fairfield, and the public libraries of New York, New Haven, Hartford, Boston. The long and persistent task of research has been a continuous pleasure, for it has revealed riches and opened associations that are full of promise.

In giving these papers to the public the author expresses the sincere desire that there will result some quickening of patriotic sentiment. It requires only the spirited play of the imagination, and these familiar places are peopled with men and women of the past engaged in strenuous and varied activities. One passes along the edges of Pequot swamp (the few remaining acres of this famous battleground ought to be converted into a little park and kept like to the days of old for the

sake of coming generations)—one passes along
the swamp, and listens almost unconsciously
for the warning notes of struggle and carnage
which once sounded through the woods. One
stands on Greenfield Hill looking down Verna
Avenue, that stretch of exquisite, shadeful
greenery, and for a moment it seems that Tal-
leyrand, who once tarried at the old inn, might
stand by one's side and gaze enraptured upon
the glorious scene, or President Dwight might
cross over the way to the observer and recite
enthusiastically some of his verses:

> " As round me here I gaze, what prospects rise,
> Ethereal, matchless ! "

One climbs the remnant of breastworks on
Grover's Hill, and it all comes back to him—the
terror of anticipated assault, the courage of
brave soldiers defending the town, the roar of
cannon, the mystery of small boats stealthily
making their way toward Ash Creek, the stir,
anxiety, sacrifice, victory, of long ago. One
leans against the ancient whipping-post on the

Fairfield Green, and again there sounds in his
ear the whiz of the lash, the cry of the culprit; the children jeer at the slave in the
stocks ; the prisoner taken from the jail is exposed to the punishment of public gaze, and
all sorts of curious transactions take place before us. It is these things and kindred expe-
riences that are evoked by the witchery of our
common imagination and the few rude lines
drawn by the writer's hand. As we live in this
strange past, may it be that some high purpose pushing into nobler patriotism shall be
communicated unto us, so that the future shall
be made the better, happier, brighter. With
the hope that men and women whose lives are
associated with the grand old New England
towns may grow strong in their devotion to
these precious nurseries of character, the author commits this book unto the tender mercies of the generous reader.

FAIRFIELD, CONN.,
September 1, 1895.

CONTENTS

ILLUSTRATIONS

xvi. ILLUSTRATIONS.

"O, who can paint like nature! who can boast
  Such scenes as here enchant the lingering eye!"

PRESIDENT DWIGHT.

I.

Woods and Plains; Hillside and Seaside.

I.

THIS particular old New England town nes-
tles down by an inflow of the sea. The fellowship of the " Sound " with Connecticut on one
side and Long Island on the other, gives infinite interest and variety to the landscape. The
Indians were charmed with this sweet enchantment of nature. Their wigwams dotted many
of the shores.

What virginal loveliness it was that painted
itself upon the eyes of the wearied immigrants
when they reached this spot ! In their first
enthusiasm we can see them turn aside from
the hard toil of rearing log cabins and cultivating patches of corn. Some lad has been on a
little tramp back to the elevation now called
Round Hill. He has found an opening in

the trees where the redman is wont to kindle his signal fires. So this brave, curious son urges the family and neighbors to come with him and see the landscape.

At length they stand in the open on the top of this commanding eminence. To the north they turn, and endless forests upon hill and in dale wave them a welcome. To the east the lands seem broken with the shimmering surfaces of little indentations from the sea. On the west there spreads out a like variegation of woodland, water-way, and small oases of cultivated fields. To the south lies the broad, shifting expanse of the Sound, reaching into the east and the west until the eyes tire of the straining. Beyond, to the farther south, lies Long Island, its many miles of forest-covered sand serving as a sort of breastwork against the too familiar approach of old ocean in its hours of tumult. Whichever way the little company on Round Hill turned, it was to lose self in the dim and shadowy distances of beautiful scenes.

Picking the way down toward the shore, we see them stopping now and then to gather bunches of wild flowers, rarely precious in their sight; and they remark upon the abundance, variety, and loveliness of the blossoms. For we must remember that these people came from a land of gardens, cathedrals, art galleries. They were men and women of refinement and culture. The beautiful must needs appeal to them; and when it was not found in artificial forms, it became all the more welcome in nature. Whatever may have been the feeling in respect to old-world beauty, however earnestly these people thrust from their mind the art-work of the mother country, the instinct and sensitiveness which enabled one to appreciate such handiwork as revealed itself in nature still remained active and fruitful.

One of the things which Ludlow and his associates did was to stake out the village. The central plat was reserved for the Green. The other squares were portioned among the new settlers. It is more than two hundred and fifty years since this work was done, but the original divisions remain virtually unchanged.

There was more or less swamp land that has been converted into garden or meadow. Trees have been felled, others placed in orderly manner, roads made and re-made according to the times, houses destroyed and houses rebuilt, all the minor changes that necessarily pertain to the life of a town; but the landscape is essentially the same that greeted the first comers.

The hand of taste and refinement has been at work through the generations. The soil has been subdued and made productive of all things agreeable to this climate and location. Yet the emotions of the early residents must have been quite like to those which stir us to-day as we look upon the matchless picture.

Visit Round Hill on a clear October morning. It is a scene that will never fade. There is the park expanse which immediately surrounds one. The hill has just enough elevation to give it dignity and command the prospect. The turf stretches beneath the feet, a mantle of

velvet verdure. The monotony is broken by
smooth, winding roads, small masses of shrub-
bery, varied trees artistically grouped.

This noble promontory is framed with a rural
setting it were hard to surpass. Farm lands and
bits of wooded territory press close beneath
the hill. Beyond is the wider adornment of
the shaded towns, north, east, west, south. The
white spire of the church in Greenfield Hill
shines in the distance. The mansion of Verna
Farm paints itself against the background of
thick foliage. Southport rests serenely down
by the edge of the water, flashing light into the
eyes from its half-hidden roofs and steeples.
Bridgeport masses its wide-spread surface beneath the gaze ; its tall chimneys, great shops,
various institutions, pleasant homes, woven into
forms that suggest busy life and manifold
works. Black Rock pushes into the sea.
Grover's Hill, crowned with its commodious
and restful country seats, imparts a touch of
subdued elegance.

Between Round Hill and the shore lie the

squares made by Ludlow. The ample proportions of the houses are barely discernible amid
the embowered streets. One catches a glimpse
of a red Norman tower, a shining band of rail-
road, now and then a roof, an occasional flag-
staff, some portion of the old Town Hall, a
dark spire, a white house-front, the straggling
rear proportions of a great brown mansion,
here and there patches of colonial yellow, an
ample and substantial brick barn half clad
with vines, vast and interesting variety of material.

And all this landscape is brightened and glo-
rified by the myriad tints of autumn. Rainbows have been woven into the whole setting of
the picture. Nature is aflame with its splendor
and brilliancy of manifestation. Meanwhile
the infinite and changeful waters of the sea
spread their charm and beauty just beyond the
old town and its neighbors, giving tone, relief,
suggestion, offset, to the gorgeous scene. Did
some one say, " See Naples and then die " ?
It were scarce worth while to ring down the cur-

tain for so small an inducement. See Fairfield from Round Hill on a perfect October day, and live.

But there is an all-year-round beauty peculiar to the place. When winter comes and nature is stripped of bright colors and gay forms, there still remains a wealth of beauty.

Walk to Osborn Hill some clear, crisp morning, after the rain has frozen upon tree, and bush, and rock. What a transformation: There are the same outlines of beauty. We see the same houses, fields, streets, shores. But every object is hung with crystal. It is a look into fairyland. Gems are scattered with such prodigality that we count them common things. The sunshine has been caught by every tiny twig and rough stone, withered blade of grass, massive tree, and bold rock. The October brilliancy has suddenly returned and assumed fresh, radiant forms. Gold, sapphire, pearl, chalcedony, all the jewels of the world's royalty, the diamonds of the African mines, the silver of Peru and Nevada—are they not scattered through the landscape, dimming the eyes with their glory?

It is always beautiful, this gem of landscape by the sea. He must be blind indeed who, taking it into his vision, does not nourish his soul upon it. Whether one tramps through the marshes in damp, gray days, studying our flora in order to write "How to Know the Wild Flowers," or lingers in field and forest on a midsummer's day to glean pictures for "The Friendship of Nature," devotees of the beautiful treasure the inspirations which come to them amid these scenes.

And like inspirations belong to you and me as we put ourselves in the mood and open our eyes to the scenes that stretch before us. This setting of nature is not an insignificant factor in the development of character and the determination of events. We have thought it well to point unto this landscape opulence, so that we might get a clearer apprehension of the men, the deeds, the spirit, the life, peculiar to this old New England town. For environment is bound to express itself in terms of manhood and action. We may therefore expect that such a landscape as has been described, as well as the many sorts of weather characteristic of these shores, and the manifold trials which sturdy pioneers must face, will contribute generously to character, destiny, achievement.

II.

Puritans and Pilgrims.

II.

THE first settlers came with a common inheritance of the best English manhood. They all submitted to a common environment of untamed wilderness, Indian peril, fickle weather, stern subsistence.

These pioneers came in three companies—the band from Windsor in 1639, the band from Watertown, and later still the band from Concord.

These Massachusetts emigrants represented three ecclesiastical tendencies. First there were the men that called themselves Independents. Plymouth and Pilgrim are the words which suggest them. There were also men that had Presbyterian preferences. And there were men who still loved the Church of England. These people were Puritans. Circumstances wrought the three classes into the Congregational form of church life.

The emigrants came from a land that was already quickened unto enlarged prosperity. Holland was doing much for England by way of teaching thrift, trade, commerce, manufacture. A new spirit of enterprise and activity was widespread. The emigrants were involved in the contagion. Comrades had been into Holland. There was intimate correspondence between the men who remained in England, the men who tarried in Holland, and the men who adventured into America. The spirit of progress prevailed among them.

The families that came to these shores were variously circumstanced. Some of them never possessed large means; others had lost through persecution the property which belonged to them; and quite a number brought a greater or less fortune with them. They all adapted themselves to circumstances with a good sense and a cheerfulness most remarkable.

We quite properly think of them as men of ideas and principles. This was their shining characteristic. It had been a rough discipline through which they had passed in the mother country. They were largely Puritans, and they insisted upon pure life, pure doctrine, pure worship. Since many of them loved the English Church, their revolt was not necessarily a revolt against it, but a revolt against corrupt practice and tyrannical method. When King James said concerning this class of people, " I will make them conform, or I will harry them out of the kingdom," he said a very foolish and cruel thing. But his foolishness and cruelty wrought to the ultimate gain and triumph of the emigrants.

Wiclif had long ago set the people of England thinking. A thinking man is like a hidden force in nature. The time comes when the ferment of thought expresses itself in the visibility and momentum of action. Contact with the enterprise and politics of little Holland served to hasten the course which events were bound to take.

2

Men of ideas, they thought for themselves. And they had thought out Church and State problems to the extent that they were prepared to move along the lines of freedom and independence.

Men of principles, they believed that righteousness was the true foundation of personal character and national life. They looked for a rule that was instinct with the spirit of God. It was their conviction that the individual possessed certain inalienable rights. They proposed to get into some land where these rights might be freely exercised. In the providence of God, Unquowa, an Indian expanse of territory by the great arm of the sea, was destined to become a nursery of such ideas and principles as were seething in the hearts and consciences of the Puritans.

Given, then, such stock as we have indicated, subject it to the training peculiar to the times, transplant it to this new-world environment, cultivate it in accordance with the hard, rigorous conditions which prevailed, and what is the result? Men that are bound to take influential and commanding part in the solution of great world problems, and make the pages of history lively with vast enterprises and noble achievements.

Roger Ludlow, the man who spied out the land which we call Fairfield, was a gentleman from Wilts County, England, a man of station, culture, force. Arrived in Massachusetts, he became at once an important factor in the conduct of public affairs, holding several offices at different times, one of them being that of deputy-governor. Disappointed, however, at the choice of Haynes and Bellingham for governor and deputy-governor in Massachusetts Colony, he was glad to turn his thought toward the settlement of Connecticut. He came to Windsor with a little company. There was trouble concerning the choice of lands. But the tasks of settlement went forward. Ludlow was a keen observer of men, one swift to measure the needs of the occasion, a thinker intent upon the wise solution of the peculiar difficulties which beset the colonists.

On January 14, 1639, all the "free plant-
ers" of the Connecticut Colony met at Hartford and adopted a constitution. Hooker had
preached his now famous sermon, in which he
asserted the right of the people to choose and
to limit the powers of their rulers, some seven
months earlier in the year. It is conceded that
the germ potentially of the colony constitution was that sermon of Hooker's. But the
mind of Ludlow also is seen by some scholars
in the important document. As one compares
it with Ludlow's Code of 1649, the evidences
seem good that the same intellect shared both
tasks.

It was while in the pursuit of hostile Pequots that the beautiful scenery and the fine
water privileges of these shores attracted the
deputy-governor. Permission being granted
him to form a settlement in this section, he
brought the first little company of pioneers to
Unquowa during the summer or fall of 1639.

Land was purchased of the Indians. Ludlow was the leading spirit, and his were the

shaping influences in the new town. There
was a certain arbitrariness and demonstrative
energy that suggested how he proposed to have
his own way. But the people associated with
him knew their own mind about things, and
they were not slow to express their sentiments
and convictions. While they were ready to
hear advice and consider propositions, they
were not the kind of men to submit to dic-
tation or to repress their opinions. Circumstances compelled all hands to work ; and while
the settlers toiled in the subjugation of the
land and the support of life, they kept their
minds busy with plans, and they carefully
weighed current ideas.

Scarcely did they rear humble places of
abode for themselves ere they chose a site for
the meeting-house, and built the rough, simple structure where they could securely house
their public worship, and frankly speak with
one another upon the great questions of faith
and practice. In this little log building the
public school was also started and the town

meetings were held. Religion, education, politics, all centred here, and the men took a
hand in the management of these diverse
spheres of activity as occasion arose for it.
When the Rev. John Joanes came to Fairfield,
in 1644, with his associates from Concord, the
prosperity of the town seemed assured, and
the brave settlers threw themselves with re-
newed zeal into making the place a strong and
influential part of the colony.

III.

Indians, Wolves, Train-bands.

III.

THE village was platted just as we see it to-day. But it was untamed wilderness. When the trees were cleared away, and the cabins made to dot the squares, it was at best a scraggy, stumpy, uneven stretch of rough acres.

But it was not long ere it assumed the appearance of comparative liveliness. The men carried their muskets with them when they worked in the field or marshalled the family to meeting. And the only safe way to go into the woods was to go in little companies properly armed.

Although a friendly spirit was manifest on the part of some Indians, yet there were other redskins that haunted the forests in order that they might surprise some thoughtless child or solitary man, and carry away a prisoner or take human life. I find the following in the journal of William Wheeler: " The Indians about Fairfield were fond of war, and often solicited the Old Chief for leave to destroy the English. Once they obtained it on condition of pulling up a large neighboring white oak tree. Well, to work they went and stript off its branches, but still the trunk baffled their utmost endeavors. 'Thus,' says the Old Sachem, 'will be the end of your war. You may kill some of their papooses, but the old plaguey stump t'other side the great waters will remain and send out more branches.' "

The tragical end which came to the warlike Pequots in the year 1637, when they had retreated to the swamp which now bears their name, was a sort of warning to the Indians of the neighborhood. They did not venture to harass the white man to any great extent.

They continued their semi-possession of territory. There were signal fires kindled as of

yore. "Samp Mortar," the curious, massive rock on the hill amid the trees, with its capacious bowl in which the corn was placed and converted into Indian meal, still served domestic purposes and gathered the tribes into its vicinity. (It remains to-day one of the most interesting relics of a by-gone age and race. On the west side of Mill River, some three miles from the Sound, eighty feet above the bed of the stream, the precipice hangs over the narrow gorge—a wild, rugged, picturesque bit of scenery, suggestive of Indian habit and character.)

Occasionally the Indians came into the settlement to trade, although such permission was granted under narrow restrictions.

Imagine how the children gazed at them with wonder or defiance, while the men watched them with a keenness and fidelity matched only by that of the savage himself.

The settlers of the town were also grievously annoyed by the wild beasts that kept stealing their provisions and domestic animals.

Nay, the wolves, the bears, the wildcats, assaulted the very people when the occasion was favorable. Many a night were these roadways travelled by the destructive and dangerous beasts. The stealthy tread, or the hungry growl, or the angry snarl sounded distinct upon the ears of the family gathered closely in the log house.

The town authorities were obliged to offer rewards for the killing of these thieving creatures.

On February 16, 1664, it was ordered "that any one who kills a wolf in the town, if he expects to be paid for it, he shall bring the wolf's head to the treasurer, who shall keep an account thereof."

It is not stated what the officer did with the interesting relics. According to accounts, he must have gathered a goodly collection in the course of years.

On August 22, 1666, " The Townsmen order that whoever kills a bear in the bounds of the town at any time between this and the next

Town meeting shall be paid out of the Town Treasury fifty shillings for each old, and for cubs twenty shillings each."

So we see that the first years in the life of the town were times of thrilling adventure. Richard Lyon would meet Captain Robert Turney and tell how he saved a sheep from the death grip of a bear. Henry Rowland and Andrew Ward would relate how they were watched by a prowling Indian who skulked behind old stumps and great trees. Nathan Gold would gather the villagers about him and narrate his journey to Hartford. Marshal Samuel Morehouse would call to mind that Pastor Hooker's wife was carried in a litter all the way from Boston to the new settlement on the Connecticut River. Roger Ludlow would tell about the preaching of Mr. Hooker, and the impression it made upon the men that went to Hartford to form a government for the colony.

When training day came everybody expected to see the sight, and enjoy a little neighborhood

leisure. It was a fine company of men that the
women and children looked upon as the drilling
was done on the village Green and up and
down the village streets. See the men in their
jerkins, small-clothes, short cloaks, steeple-
crowned hats. The muskets and the long pikes
were the favorite weapons, with belt for sword
and cartridge-boxes. The soldiers often wore
quilted coats or iron breast-plates as a protection against the arrows of the enemy.

On the training days of 1653 the people of
Fairfield discussed the perils of war with the
Dutch. England and Holland were not on
friendly terms, and it was rumored that the
Dutch from New Amsterdam proposed to pass
up the Sound and capture the shore towns.
What with wringing a living from the soil, put-
ting up decent buildings, killing off the wild
beasts, guarding against the sly assaults of
Indians, keeping up communication with neighboring settlements, it was a very toilsome and
perilous life. And now the encroachment of
the Dutch was added to their difficulties.

Feeling upon this latter subject was intense and bitter. The General Court of Connecticut, in March, 1654, ordered the arrest of Thomas Baxter, of Fairfield, for disturbing the peace of the colony. He proposed to move immediately against the enemy. He gathered a little company about him, and seized a vessel off these shores, for the purpose of attacking the Dutch.

When arrested and tried for such conduct, it was testified in court here by John Odell, that, "as Baxter's men went up and down the streets of Fairfield with their swords drawn in their hands, he heard William Ellitt swear with a great oath (but knows not the words) that with them hands of his he would be avenged upon the blood of some of them which had taken his captain ; and he supposed there was about a dozen of them which so run with their swords drawn."

It would create something of excitement to see to-day a dozen men rushing along our streets shouting vengeance and brandishing swords. Doubtless the excitement was widespread two hundred and forty-one years ago. But peace was declared between England and Holland in 1654, so that the war cloud lifted.

It must have been an interesting scene, two years later, when in April there assembled in Fairfield the chief sachems of the neighboring Indians, that they might take counsel with the white brothers concerning the sale of these familiar acres. Although Ludlow had paid for the land which he distributed among the new settlers, the Indians still felt that they had claims upon it.

This April meeting of 1656 was to decide the matter. A new sale was made, the deed signed by various prominent individuals, and a large quantity of cloth, pots, kettles, looking-glasses, scissors, knives, hatchets, hoes, and spades passed into the possession of the friendly Indians of Pequonnock and Unquowa.

And now many questions came to the court and community for settlement. Ludlow had left Fairfield in high dudgeon, and yielded his

efficient leadership to whomsoever circumstances and the choice of the people might
elect (which ultimately signified the leadership of Nathan Gold).

There were questions about land, management of the Indians, adjustment of boundaries,
laying out of highways; discussion concerning
the Golden Hill reservation, and the rights of
the Pequonnocks. Things sacred and things
secular, matters political and matters ecclesiastical, they came indiscriminately into church
meetings and town meetings, so that it was
hard to say whether the church was running
the town, or the town was running the church.

It was a difficult task which the Rev. John
Joanes had in hand, the shepherding of such a
flock. Edward Johnson, in his book entitled,
" Wonder Working Providence of Zion's Sav-
ior," gives us a sonnet upon the subject:

" In Desart's Depths where Wolves & Beares abide
Thou Joanes sits down a weary watch to keepe
O'er Christ's deare flock, who now are wandered
wide."

3

But the reverend scholar did very good service, and retained the love and confidence of his people to the day of death.

When Governor Ludlow took his departure there was genuine sorrow and disappointment on the part of many citizens; but the sturdy manhood of the people asserted itself, and life flowed along according to the accustomed way with its usual variety of adventure and hard labor.

The Rev. Samuel Wakeman, successor to Mr. Joanes, threw himself with all zeal into the private and public affairs of the community. In addition to Major Gold he found such co-workers as Captain John Burr and his brother Jehu. It was a sad and singular circumstance that these four men died the same year, and caused a widespread mourning that was very deep and impressive.

The mention of death calls to mind the fact that the bodies of these faithful citizens were deposited in the " Burial Hill " (just beyond the present residence of Mr. Henry S. Glover), in accordance with the custom of the times, without any religious services. Mourning rings and garments were quite elaborate those days. So that the whole community must have been plunged into the gloom of death emblems and etiquette.

Major Gold was succeeded by his already famous son, Nathan the Second. The Rev. Joseph Webb, who pronounced the interesting, all-day-long sermon of commemoration in honor of Major Gold, had been installed in place of the departed Pastor Wakeman, while one and another efficient and intelligent citizen lent a hand to the tasks of common, public interest.

Fairfield was the centre of numerous preparations for war. It being the shire town, and later the half-shire town, affairs naturally took their rise in the place. We read various statements in the town records concerning the purchase of arms, the days of training, the tax for support of militia, the assault of Indian, Dutch, and French foes.

Something of the kind continued down to the ending of the American Revolution. The martial spirit became native to the soil. The means and measures of war were as thoroughly canvassed as the condition of the crops. Boys gave their play a soldier character with an instinct like to that which drives ducks into the water. Life was such a rigorous and uncertain experience, the town was such a conspicuous mark for all sorts of attack, the times were so restless and eventful, it must needs be that the people who walked these streets and tilled these acres looked upon things with a constitutional seriousness that almost repels their modern successors.

If we to-day were circumstanced as were these brave and toilsome people two hundred years ago, afraid that wolves or bears might steal our animals or attack our children, watchful lest savages or white men might suddenly make an onset by land or by sea and destroy the village, burdened with the cares and labors peculiar to pioneer conquest, it is quite probable that our

manner of speech and spirit of life would show
a like gravity.

And then there was not a little friction between adjoining towns.   Dispute after dispute
arose, and these wise, earnest men did their
best to settle matters.   We find so much concerning these small misunderstandings that one
is inclined to   exaggerate their   importance.
But closer examination shows us that they were
largely the matters that grew out of the new-
ness of the country and the satisfactory or
unsatisfactory distribution of the lands.

Communication with sister towns and the
great centres of life was by means of post-horses.
It was an exciting time when John Perry, the
carrier of the mail, the man of news, the individual who kept Fairfield in touch with Boston,
Stamford, and intervening towns, arrived and
handed over mail and news together.   He was
appointed to office in 1687.   The whole trip was
made once a month during the winter, and
once in three weeks during the summer.   He
was an important person, a trusty man, one that

was compelled to thread many perils and show considerable wit and discretion in his journeys.

As he trots along the street, we can see one after another of the citizens hastening down to the inn where his horse is changed, or to the little office where the mail is distributed. The venerable pastor of the Prime Ancient Society or the respected deputies who represent the town in the General Court at Hartford will not consider it beneath their dignity to walk with quickened step down to the meeting-place in order that they may put to Goodman John Perry a few straight questions concerning the trend of events and the weal of the colonies.

It was during the latter years of the seventeenth century that Captain Kidd was sent forth to do service against the pirates, and turned biggest pirate of all himself. He sailed about these waters for some years. As his adventures were carried from mouth to mouth, we know something about the feeling here in Fairfield when it was learned that he had been depositing treasure in various places about the neighborhood. While his piracy was stamped with strongest condemnation, yet a justifiable curiosity was here manifest, and many were the suppositions current in respect to his sudden advent in this region and his cunning concealment of enormous treasure.

IV.

Domestic Affairs.

IV.

THE ebb and flow of life in the old country influenced to a considerable extent the social conditions of New England. But the colonists themselves were of course the important factors in the significant transitions of the times. Fairfield being the heart of county business, it resulted that every question and event of the day was discussed with a thoroughness characteristic of our thoughtful people. When some brawler was put into the stocks on the Green, the children would gather about the culprit and investigate him. When legal matters drew the men of the county or colony to town, the older people gathered in much the same way to know the thing at issue with them.

Strict regulations governed the sale of liquors at the little inn. No profanity was permitted among the citizens. Idlers were set to work or driven from the town. The moral tone of the community was excellent. Even the slaves (for slavery prevailed to an extent in Fairfield) behaved themselves generally with decency and quietness. There was considerable traffic carried on at this time, although the people's wants were comparatively few and the number of commodities quite limited.

The first pressure of settlement and conquest had passed. The small cabins had been replaced by frame houses. A new meeting-house forty feet square, clapboarded, with tower in centre, had been constructed.

The surrounding forests were grown thin in places where meadow and pasture had been laid out. The vegetable gardens flourished with their variety of products. Sheep, cattle, swine, fowls, made the town lively and musical with their presence. The children went short distances into the neighboring fields, and along the borders of the woods, to pick the abundant berries. Fruit trees were cultivated, and helped to supply the people with food and drink. The town prospered and grew influential through the colony.

Meanwhile, the usual changes of temperature, severe storms, and natural phenomena peculiar to the coasts of this lower New England, made their record.

Mr. Webb notes several tornadoes and earthquakes. "On the 23d of May, 1700," he writes, "there happened a most prodigious tempest in Fairfield, of wind, rain, thunder, hail. . . . We had four beds wet very considerably, and were forced to move into the entry to secure ours from the water which ran down in great abundance in both the lower rooms. . . . There fell also very great hail stones as big as a hen's eggs. 'Tis said that one of them taken up was as big as a goose egg. . . . The wind overturned and destroyed twenty barns. . . . Most of the barns in the way of it that fell not were more or less dam-

nifyed by it. . . . It took off the roof of one
house endways and took off a good part of the
chimney with it. . . . It blew down abundance
of trees in the woods. The violence of the
storm lasted not above three minutes as was
considered."

This seems to have been a time of marked
atmospheric disturbances. Mr. Webb notes
others. "On Friday, June 6, sun about an
hour and a half high in the afternoon, there
was a noise in the air (as was supposed) like
the report of a great gun, very smart, as if two
had been fired. . . .

"April 30. About noon we were sensible of
an earthquake in Fairfield, which was very considerable. . . . May 4. Between nine and ten
of the clock at night we had another earthquake, which was also taken notice of at Norwalk."

Another storm broke above Fairfield about
this time. "It shook the Bible out of the
hand of John Baylies, numbed his arm, killed
a dog that was lying under a chair where the

children were sitting. . . ." Still another earthquake. "The glass rattled in ye windows, and
ye floor seemed to tremble under my feet for
some time in ye lower room, and some that
were in ye garret perceived ye house to shake
and heard a rumbling noise."

These interesting notes are found upon the
manuscript of the sermon preached by Mr.
Webb in commemoration of Major Gold. The
cost and scarcity of paper compelled them to
practise rigid economy in its use.

The same word which Mr. Webb employs
to describe the harm done by the first storm
mentioned seems quite expressive when we
call to mind some of the recent storms which
have visited us. "Damnifyed" is emphatic
and comprehensive.

But an examination of the record leads us to
believe that the cold was intenser, the snows
deeper, and the winters harder in the olden
times than during the modern. Certain marked
changes seem to have come to the New England climate and seasons alongshore which

suggest that we have moved south into Vir-
ginia.

And now let us look upon a rough sketch of
the seven calendar days. First comes Monday. The traveller starts on his journey. The
farmer goes bright and early to his work. The
children are sent off to school. The gudewife
and her helper attend to the washing, and
soon the yards of the town are adorned with
spotless linen fluttering in the breezes. The
family fares humbly on this day; but appe-
tite is good, so that any food is taken with
a relish. And the day ends, as it begins, with
family worship; then a speedy retirement to
bed.

Tuesday dawns upon a busy scene. There is
more or less baking to do, and the week's iron-
ing is also on hand. But the town is alive
with men from neighboring settlements. It is
the day when the court holds a session. Lawyers, clients, witnesses, crowd the town "Ordinary," and the citizens interested in the matters under consideration leave their work for a

few hours and tarry in the neighborhood of the Town Hall.

Everybody is concerned in the business of the court. It has to do with the prosperity and character of the town. Probably some new object of judicial penalty is put behind the bars of the small jail. It may be that the whipping-post is brought into service, and the Green becomes the scene of a lashing bestowed upon a wife-beater, or a lying slave, or a boisterous ne'er-do-well.

Wednesday is mid-week, and most important. This is lecture day. Boston seems to have set the fashion, and Fairfield kept in close touch with this capital city of New England; although in Boston Thursday was preferred to Wednesday for the mid-week lecture. Work is put one side, and the family is marshalled to the meeting-house.

The service is much like the Sabbath order. Mr. Wakeman or Mr. Webb may take occasion to speak with greater frankness than on Sunday concerning matters that are more personal.

4

The custom of painting the face has been imported into Boston, and some one of course brings the fashion into this progressive neighborhood. We know of one faithful pastor in New England who told his people " that at the resurrection of the Just there will no such sight be met as the Angels carrying painted Ladies in their arms." We are to think of such practical matters being discussed with great candor and directness on Wednesday.

Then the politics of the day give frequent opportunity for forcible lecture talks. This occasion seems all the more favorable for such addresses, since immediately after service, with a slight intermission perchance for quenching the thirst with cider and breaking the fast upon doughnuts and pie, the men hold their town meeting.

Due warning having been given, Wednesday after lecture is a very convenient time for the transaction of local business. " At Town meeting April 29th, 1665, it was voted that upon Wednesday every fortnight after the

conference meeting, there shall be a townsmen's meeting for the attentions of the Town's
occasions."

Fast Day services and Thanksgivings were
generally appointed on this day in Connecticut. Occasionally court held sessions at the
time. A sermon preceded the opening of
court. In 1651 court adjourned to " meet on
second Lecture Day in March, Wednesday,
after sermon."

Thursday was on occasion a very lively day.
The workers now saw their way through the
week. Large portion of the toil had been
done. A certain freedom and relaxation of
life were manifest. Perhaps the militia trained.
Gingerbread and home-brewed drinks were
prepared in great abundance. Arms were put
into bright condition. Clothes were brushed
and mended. Everybody appeared spick
and span clean. The drum-beat sounded
through the streets and echoed back from
the neighboring forests.

All the people that could leave their homes

and walk the streets or stand about the Green were on hand to admire the men of the town; and everybody that stayed at home kept running to the small window or the open door to watch the sturdy company as it bravely passed up and down the lively way.

Frequent refreshment and the admiration of on-lookers stimulated the train-band to do its level best. When the day ended there came over the people of Fairfield a consciousness that as manly a company of soldiers were at the command of the colony for warfare offensive and defensive as could be found in New England.

Friday was the time when the hard work of the week was further relaxed, and friends might drop in upon each other and have supper together. Occasionally there would be a wolf hunt. The swamp down in the salt meadows was one favorite lurking-place of these pestiferous creatures. The men would surround the swamp, beat up the brutes, and then enjoy the excitement of a chase and a capture.

Or it might be some fishing expedition which
was appointed.   Sea food made an important
part of the daily fare here in town.   It enabled
the people to get comfortably through many a
season when crops were scant and provisions
low.

Friday was a good day for the boys to carry
the corn down to the old mill by the river.
This was a pleasant outing for them, and there
was opportunity to tell their latest adventures
and gather any fresh local news.

Or this might be the day when, as was voted
in 1670, every male " from fourteen years old
and upwards, except assistants, commissioners,
or ministers of the gospel, shall work one day
annually in cutting brush and making public
pasture."

Saturday was a sort of preparation day.
There was more baking, fixing best frocks, setting the house in order, gathering up the threads
of work for the week, and bringing everything
into the best condition possible.

The many things to be done in a rural com-

munity like Fairfield, during these days, kept
repeating themselves over and over again as
the weeks went by. Certain kinds of food
must be cooked on this day. A generous stock
of provision must be stored for the Sabbath.
All labor must end at sundown. The family
must be quietly settled at home. No noise of
any kind was permitted upon the street when
the evening had set in. Supper, study of the
Bible, reading of an occasional religious book,
worship, and early rest—that was the way Saturday ended.

Sunday was the great day of the week.
When breakfast was done and the family had
joined in worship, every one prepared for meeting. The drum-beat sounded, and the streets
were lively for a few minutes with the little
companies marching off to the meeting-house
on the Green.

The first bell was put into the tower or belfry
in 1685. "At a Town meeting held April 28th,
1685, it was voted, that the townsmen should
settle Samuel Wilson's matter, about satisfying

him for money the Town borrowed of him to pay for the meeting-house bell."

All having assembled, a guard was placed before the door in order that the congregation might not be surprised or overpowered by the Indians. Mr. John Gold "gets and reads the psalm," as the church records phrase it. Then Mr. Wakeman or Mr. Webb, having set the hour-glass, proceeded with the service. It was long. But the patience of the people was longer.

At noon the congregation adjourned to the Green, or to the Sabbath-day house if it was winter. They ate their simple lunches and drank their favorite cider, and as the drum-beat sounded again they once more assembled in the meeting-house.

The second service was like unto the first. The minister frequently continued the same theme that he considered in the morning. He was bound to be thorough in the matter. And when the citizens had enjoyed some five hours of this sort of thing they were kindly dismissed and permitted to go home and eat a cold dinner. The Green and the streets were deserted the rest of the day.

Evening drawing on apace, the men might have been seen attending to their cattle.   Then the inhabitants were shut into their homes for the night, and the rest-day had done for them its helpful and peculiar service.   Did an Indian, a wild beast, or a traveller appear upon the scene during the day, there was a momentary excitement until such time as the intruder was suppressed.   But the abiding characteristic of the Lord's Day in Fairfield, as in other Puritan towns, was a decorum, silence, repose, simply phenomenal.

The records give us a fair idea of the well-to-do homes of Fairfield during this first century.

The house of Mr. Webb was a good example: a frame building with quite substantial doors, small windows with little panes of glass, the entry in the middle of the structure, living-room on the one side, "best" room on the other, kitchen extending along the rear; a second

story to the structure with several narrow bed-rooms.

Wills and inventories tell us how the house was furnished. The floors were carpetless, the rugs and Turkey cloths being used for the covering of tables. There were no pictures to adorn the walls. The rafters were generally visible. Natural wood was seen on every side, although some sort of tapestry was sometimes used, and various chintzes and calicoes were made into curtains and hangings.

The living-room had its tables large and small, claw-footed, and made from some solid wood. There were cupboards, stools, a few chairs, the spinning-wheel, brass candlesticks in which fish oil was first used and later spermaceti and tallow.

There was a great fireplace (Parson Daven-port, of New Haven, had thirteen in his house; his son, the Rev. John, of Stamford, married Martha, daughter of Major Gold). In the fire-place were the andirons; the bellows hung by the side, and the warming-pan was close by.

Then there were strewn about the room, or hung upon the walls, the armor, weapons, skins, antlers, which testified to the active life of the men in the defence of their homes or the pursuit of game; although the town soon passed laws restraining or forbidding the destruction of the deer, whose meat at the first had been one of their chief supports.

The other rooms of the house were sparsely furnished. A half-headed bedstead was placed in the room opposite the living-room ; it had curtains, valances, a feather or wool or down bed upon a hard bottom of boards. There were sheets, quilts, counterpanes, bolsters.

It was a cold experience, that which came to the family on a severe winter's night. One does not wonder that they felt the need of flip, a cider preparation into which a hot flatiron was thrown in order to make it steam and sizzle.

Cotton Mather tells how in 1697, as he sat before the great fire in his fireplace, " the juices forced out of the billets of wood by the heat of the flame on which they were laid, yet froze

into ice on their coming out." Another observer writes that the " bread was frozen at the
Lord's table." Yet it was a life accompanied
by infinite satisfaction. Few were the complaints, and many the fascinations.

Love-making itself was never more interesting. In some parts of Connecticut, courtship
was all done in the living-room among the family. A whispering-rod, hollow so that the
lovers could speak through it, was put into
their hands. Seated some distance apart, they
poured their billing and cooing into the pipe.

But greater freedom was granted them in
Fairfield. Sunday night being only half sacred,
it was largely devoted to this important business.

When Samuel Wakeman, the minister's son,
courted Mary, daughter of Jehu Burr, they
had all the liberties of the living-room.

To be sure, the rest of the family kept an
eye upon them. There was to be no such scene
as that in New Haven (1660), when Jacob Mur-
line went into the room where Sarah Tuttle

was, and first seized her gloves, then kissed her,
although, " being asked in court if Jacob in-
veigled her affection, she said, ' No,' " so that
the Court fined Sarah rather than Jacob, and
called her a " Bould Virgin," to which Sarah
replied, "that she hoped God would enable
her to carry it better for time to come."

There was nothing of this kind. Samuel and
Mary were discreet and strictly attentive to the
requirements of Fairfield etiquette. Matters
were quietly arranged, and when their names
had been read in public the proper number of
times, they invited their friends together, the
magistrate made them one, and they set up
housekeeping for themselves.

V.

Witchcraft and Witches.

V.

WITCHCRAFT AND WITCHES.

IT was at this period that there swept through the country a curious epidemic brought from the old world by some of these honest, sincere, godly people.

Hundreds and thousands of men, women, and children had suffered and died by reason of the witchcraft craze in England and on the Continent. When it struck the new land, it seemed for a time that it must prevail with like havoc here.

The first outbreak in Fairfield was only a few years after the settlement of the place. One tragic death was the result of the trouble at that time.

We are justified in saying that human nature manifested the characteristics common to all

ages during these early, strenuous days. When
Thomas Staples brought suit against Roger
Ludlow for defamation of his gudewife's character, the evidence in court was spiced with
much hot, strong speech. Mrs. Nathan Gold
testified, that, in a quarrel in the meeting-
house, she heard the accused woman ask Ludlow to " show her where she had told one lie ;
and Mr. Ludlow had said she need not mention particulars, for she had gone on a tract of
lying."

This poor woman was supposed by some of
the people to be a witch. But the suit brought
by her husband against Ludlow was decided
in her favor. " Considering the nature of
the charge, and Mrs. Staples's relation to the
church in Fairfield," it was ordered, by way
of sentence, "that Mr. Ludlow pay Thomas
Staples, towards repairing his wife's name so
defamed, with trouble and charge in prosecution, the sum of ten pounds."

Now, while this seemed to settle the business, the imputation of witchcraft still lingered.

In 1692 the second outbreak is recorded.
Four women were indicted, one of them being
the same person that Roger Ludlow said had
" gone on a tract of lying."

What a curious scene it is which presents
itself! The governor, the deputy-governor,
and assistants have come down to Fairfield to
attend the trial. The excitement in the town
is intense. Had they not foes enough to fight
without meeting Satan and his emissaries in
human form ?

One can imagine the terror of the children,
when parents spake guardedly and in whispers
about the fresh perils that surrounded them.

One can see how all the lore of the subject
was discussed, and everybody made to feel
some indefinable dread, lest the loud and angry
winds that bore down upon the place, or the
scurrying shadows which had a way of flitting
through the streets and along the Green by
night, might not be the actual voices and
movements of these strange, awful creatures.
The town was profoundly agitated.

5

The charge against Mercy Disborow runs as follows: "Mercy Disborow, wife of Thomas Disborow of Compo, Fairfield, thou art here indicted by the name of Mercy Disborow, that not having the fear of God before thine eyes, thou hast had familiarity with Satan, the grand enemy of God and men, and that by his instigation and help, thou hast in a preternatural way afflicted and done harm to the bodies and estates of sundry of their Majesties' subjects, or to some of them, contrary to the peace of our sovereign Lord and Lady the King and Queen, their crown and dignity; and that on the 25th of April of their Majesties' reign, and at sundry other times, by which by the laws of God and the Colony thou doest best to die. Fairfield, September 15, 1692."

Among the witnesses on this trial was one Edward Jesop. The following is his testimony, or a part of it, and a fair sample of other testimony adduced at the trial:

"Being at Thomas Disborow's house at Compo, I saw a pig roasting that looked very well, but when it came to the table (where we had a good light) it seemed to me to have no skin upon it and looked strangely; but when said Disborow began to cut it, the skin (to my apprehension) came upon it again. . . .

"She brought a Bible that was very large print to me, to read the particular Scripture; but though I had a good light and looked directly upon the book, I could not see one letter; but looking upon it again when in her hand, after she had turned over a few leaves, I could see to read above a yard off."

The same night, going home and coming to Compo Creek, "it seemed to be high water." He then proceeds to say that when he tried to shove off his canoe, it stuck in the mud "and appeared to be low water." Then he wandered all night trying to get home.

Now, such an experience to-day would scarcely be laid at the door of witchcraft. When a man sees double and sees single, and sees that it is high tide and low tide in the same minute, and sees all sorts of queer things and curious transformations, we are prone to think that he is " half seas over ; " but this was the kind of testimony that helped to convict poor Mercy Disborow.

The evidence, quite voluminous, was taken ; the case given to the consideration of the jury ; but when it came to a matter of verdict, the jury failed to agree.

Interest in the matter continued. The accusation and the details of the witch work were known to the whole community. A feeling prevailed, that while there was something mysterious about the thing, yet there might be less than was generally supposed.

At the second trial two hundred depositions were taken. The charges, which seem to us indescribably absurd, were sustained by all sorts of curious and amusing testimony.

At the conclusion of one trial the plan was adopted of throwing the women into a pond of water, and giving them a chance to sink and thus show that they were not witches, or float and prove the rightness of the verdict. This test was applied with indifferent results ; people were not satisfied.

Four witnesses swore " that Mercy Disborow, being bound hand and foot and put into the water, swam like a cork, though one labored to press her down ; " evidently the " one " being some interested person who wanted proof, by her sinking, that she was not a witch.

However, sentence of death was passed upon this poor woman by the governor. But the witchcraft contagion had abated to such extent that people were reluctant to see such sentence executed.

This, I believe, was the last case passed upon by the Connecticut judges. A better mind was coming to men, and Fairfield had always been slow to move in these matters. At length a petition was presented to the General Assembly in behalf of Mercy Disborow, and her life was spared.

Thus ended one of the startling and tragical episodes in the life of this town ; an episode, however, which, while revealing the force of a

prevalent superstition, testifies quite as distinctly to the prevailing common-sense of the
community.

We are all prepared to say that it was no
humdrum, prosaic, monotonous life which the
people of Fairfield lived during the first century
of the town's existence. There may have been
little glitter and ostentation about it, and yet
there was a tone, impulse, activity, which spake
conclusively concerning personal and colonial
worth, power, manhood, womanhood.

The forefathers and the foremothers did their
work well. The foundations which they laid
were deep and strong in righteousness, liberty,
intelligence, industry.

Many compensations came to them when
engaged in their hard, exacting tasks. The
felt presence of God, the hope that rises above
every besetment, the calm assurance that a
great destiny shall unfold to the glory of a
people and the praise of the Almighty, the
abiding consciousness that the true and the real
belong to them, and their successors shall look

upon its fruition—these were the compensations that multiplied and made life, with all its penury, danger, strenuousness, a thing of sweetness and joy to the Puritan pioneers of this old New England town.

VI.

Things Sacred and Things Secular.

VI.

MRS. JANE G. AUSTIN, the novelist, speaks of an eminent Fairfield minister in her story of "Dr. Le Baron and his Daughters." As he takes important part in the period which we now sketch, we will call to mind the incidents narrated by Mrs. Austin.

Mr. Hobart, a young theologue of Harvard, was engaged to Miss Priscilla Thomas, of Marshfield. Her father opposed the match. At the same time John Watson, of Plymouth, sought Priscilla's hand, and Noah Hobart heard of it. John Watson was well-to-do, and the young divinity student was poor. So unselfish Noah Hobart advised Priscilla Thomas to accept John Watson. Although somewhat miffed at this suggestion of her lover, she proceeded in time to act upon his advice. And wise Mr. Hobart soon comforted his heart by a marriage with Ellen Sloss, " a very pretty girl with a very pretty purse " as Mrs. Austin puts it.

It was not long before John Watson died. His widow married Isaac Lothrop. " Then Mrs. Hobart died, and Isaac Lothrop died, and at last these two [Priscilla and Noah] stood face to face with only three graves and some thirty years between them." Then they were married, while Nathaniel Lothrop, Mrs. Hobart's son, also married Ellen Hobart, Mr. Hobart's daughter.

The silver font used in the service of baptism by the First Church for a hundred years and more was the gift of Dr. Lothrop in honor of his wife Ellen Hobart.

Noah Hobart was the leader of thought here in Fairfield for a generation. Later in the century his son became eminent in the State of New York, serving the public as justice of the Supreme Court of the State, and then receiving an election to the United States Senate.

He inherited much of his father's intellectual power. It was hard battle which Mr. Hobart was compelled to do when pastor of the old church.

Mr. Webb, his predecessor, had served faithfully. Many things of importance occurred during his pastorate.

The church records tell us that on March 4, 1716, the Rev. Joseph Webb baptized Aaron Burr. The family then lived at what was called the Upper Meadow, within the portion of the parish known as Greenfield. It was a long distance which many of the worshippers came in their attendance upon divine service here in Fairfield.

The neighborhood of Pequonnock had received permission from the General Court to hold separate services in the year 1692, although the Strathfield church was not organized until 1695. In 1711 Bankside had become a separate parish.

A little later Greenfield petitioned for a church organization. The request puts the

matter quaintly: "Not only ourselves are frequently obliged to be absent from divine worship, but our poor children are under a kind of
necessity of perishing for lack of vision."

The family of Aaron Burr was one of those
described by this petition. Nevertheless, the
child and youth Aaron seemed to develop with
great promise, and the matter of church attendance and gospel influence contributed its share
to his noble, consecrated character.

If there was any one of this branch of the
family in danger of perishing for lack of vision,
it was assuredly not Aaron Burr, Sr. The
phrase fittingly describes the state of Aaron, Jr.,
son of President Burr.

The colonel was a frequent visitor in these
parts, and he makes frequent references to
"Uncle Thaddeus Burr," who had matrimonial
plans for the man who was to take such prominent and tragic part in the early events of our
national life.

It is interesting to note that later in life,
when Aaron Burr, Sr., was settled as pastor of

a Presbyterian church in Newark, N. J., he sold the old homestead to cousins of the Bradley name. One of these cousins, Joseph Bradley, was the great-grandfather of the Hon. Joseph P. Bradley, late justice of the Supreme Court of the United States.

Mr. Webb had joined with nine other ministers of Connecticut and founded Yale College. This action expressed the sentiment of his people in Fairfield. They wanted an institution for the higher education of youth, and their pastor was prepared to assist in the work.

It was felt that the work of the Christian ministry could not be efficiently performed without such help. For the times had changed. The religious sentiment was not as strong in this and other communities of New England as it had been during the first century of settlement. An element that seemed more or less antagonistic to religion had crept into the colony.

There was a great deal of discussion in respect to citizenship and church membership. Some of the colonies had settled it one way by giving the ballot only to members of the established church. Others gave it to men irrespective of the fact whether they were full members of the church or not. Then the Half-way Covenant was introduced.

The chief concern in respect to the examination of Mr. Webb, when he was installed pastor of the church in Fairfield, centred in his views upon this practice. Shall the children of baptized parents not members of the church be baptized?

The Half-way Covenant declared that baptized children, when they reached the years of discretion, must own the covenant and become formal members of the church, although they might feel that they were not prepared to come to the communion. This gave them a vote in the church, and enabled them to have their children baptized.

This was the view of Mr. Webb and the Fairfield church. It helps us to understand

why the actual membership of the church was
so small through the first two centuries of the
" Prime Ancient Society."

We also see at once a reason for the deca-
dence of spirituality in the church. The very
strictness and sobriety of Puritanism was instru-
mental, perhaps, to a degree, in producing
a reaction against the early life of the colonists.

When it was evident that some such reaction had really set in, and the moral tone of
this and other towns was lowered, our people
tried to resist these and similar encroachments
by ecclesiastical pressure of the churches
wrought into the form of the Consociation.

It was in 1708 that the General Court directed
the churches of each county to send pastor
and delegate to the county seat, and there consider the best system of church order. These
assemblies elected representatives, who went
to Saybrook and decided the matter in debate
for the whole colony. The church here was
not represented at the Saybrook meeting, but

6

it loyally accepted the platform and became one of its most earnest champions.

The Fairfield interpretation of the Saybrook articles was strict and narrow. The church seemed to incline toward Presbyterianism.

During his day Mr. Hobart labored faithfully in his efforts to uphold and encourage the ecclesiastical authority of Consociation. All that could be said in favor of such a system seemed to be said by him. The times were such that it was necessary every effort should be put forth for the help of the people into a better, stronger life.

And while the matter of Consociation was a prominent question, the presence of Episcopacy and its fair prospects of growth disturbed the orthodox, conservative citizens. 'It never rains but it pours," is a saying that was illustrated by prevailing religious conditions. Here in Fairfield for a time the atmosphere was emphatically religious—religious in the sense that moral, ecclesiastical, and theological questions and activities were uppermost in the minds of the leading people. Mr. Hobart took a large part in these discussions, publishing several small books upon one or other of them.

References have been made to the indifferent state of religion during this period. The defection of Mr. Johnson, of Yale College, and his ordination to the Episcopal ministry, created not a little feeling and not a little interest in this community.

A petition was presented to the Court on May 14, 1725, asking that an assistant might be appointed to serve with Mr. Webb here in the parish. As the petitioners express it, they desired "that their sorrowful and sinking circumstances might be relieved." The brethren that inclined to the Church of England felt that the presence of that venerable organization in town would straighten out the moral and religious tangle of affairs both public and private.

Mr. Johnson, rector in Stratford, fluctuating between that town and this in his ministry,

said that the people here were just ripe for the
transferrence of their affections to the Church
of England. Nevertheless when Dr. Laborie,
a French physician of some eminence, moved to
Fairfield in 1723, he found it was no easy task
to organize worship according to that way.

He came to this country as a teacher, under
the patronage of the Bishop of London, and
he had a hard time of it. He bought a place
of Isaac Jennings, known as "the stone house
on the rocks," which he says in a letter he had
"destinated to the service of the Church of
England." In this house he read the service,
but it was "up-hill work" for a time.

He tells us that he was "disturbed by Indians
in the vicinity of Boston," and when he came
to Fairfield "he was interrupted (in worship)
immediately by one of the magistrates." This
was on the principle of tit-for-tat.

The Independent in the mother country
must conform to Episcopacy. The Episcopalian in the daughter country must conform
to Independency. But these brethren in Fair-

field " stuck to their knitting," to use a homely phrase, and in 1724, probably, a separate Episcopal parish was organized.

On November 10, 1725, the Thanksgiving Day of that year for Connecticut, Mr. Johnson opened the new church here, and it was called Trinity Church.

This task of introducing Episcopacy was a difficult one, as the town records show. May 15, 1727, a petition to the Court at Hartford says that ten of the Fairfield Episcopalians had been lately imprisoned for non-payment of taxes to support the Congregational church.

The church building probably stood on Mill Plain. The first rector or missionary was Mr. Caner, who came to his work in 1727.

Although Mr. Johnson had said that "the whole town would embrace the Church if they had a good minister at Fairfield," he did not prove a trustworthy prophet. Mr. Caner was a good minister—an exceedingly good one. He did eminent service here. After many years of arduous toil he felt obliged to go to a smaller and less exacting parish.

So in 1747 he removed to Boston and took charge of the famous King's Chapel. He passed from the more important parish of Fairfield to the less exacting parish of King's Chapel, Boston, as he puts it, "not so much out of any lucrative views as out of regard to the weakness of his constitution, which had become unequal to the duties of the large mission of Fairfield."

This amuses us, and flatters our pride and self-esteem. Boston put second to Fairfield! But it will be in order to state, by way of friendly enlightenment, that Mr. Caner's parish was rather large, compassing, at times, Greenfield, the Southport territory, Green's Farms, Pequonnock, Westport, Norwalk, Stamford, Greenwich, Redding, Ridgefield, Danbury, Weston, Wilton, New Canaan, and other like suburbs of Fairfield.

Mr. Caner started with twelve communicants and some forty families, in 1727, as he testifies in his correspondence, and they, he says, "were mostly of the poorer sort." A great change, you see, since the first days. That is the last phrase in all the world that we should think of using to describe our Episcopalian neighbors to-day—"mostly of the poorer sort." All the more honor to Mr. Caner for that fact, and for his frank truthfulness in stating it.

One feels quite sure that Oxford University did a just thing when she made this earnest, faithful worker a doctor of divinity; and we are told that he was received in England "with the respect which he so well deserved as the father of the American clergy."

When he went to Boston the church here had grown from the twelve communicants to two hundred. Sixty-eight of them actually lived in this village.

Meanwhile theological controversy had waxed hot in the colony, and Fairfield was one storm centre. One is led to suspect that so much time and attention were given to the exterior aspects and circumstances of religion that the inner life was somewhat neglected. While Mr. Caner and Mr. Hobart both labored faithfully for the cure of souls, we are constrained to think that politics, dogma, law, business, kept the people of this old New England town absorbed to such extent that spiritual life became stagnant and uninteresting.

Thirteen years after starting their organization here, the Trinity people built a new sanctuary on the land now belonging to the Rowland homestead.

The town voted on July 27, 1738, that "Liberty to the members of the Church of England" be granted "to erect a house for public worship on the highway near Old Field Gate." The structure was fifty-five feet in length, thirty-five feet in width, and twenty feet in height. The spire shot one hundred feet into the air. A bell weighing five hundred pounds was put into the belfry.

Episcopalians who lived within a mile of this edifice were granted the privilege of paying their taxes to the support of worship in this sanctuary. Other Episcopalians were for a long time compelled to pay their taxes to the support of the Congregational church.

At this time the town was a port of entry; court business increased; shops and stores multiplied; wealth, culture, fashion, exerted wide influence. A certain leadership was won and sustained by Fairfield. Lieutenant-Governor Gold, active in affairs, had finished his honorable life record. Prominent men of the colonies were frequent or occasional guests. Relations with neighbor towns and distant cities were quite intimate. It was a period of signal prosperity, and future prospects never seemed brighter.

The French war interested the citizens, for the people of Fairfield were always prepared to play a conspicuous part in encounters of this kind. It was Colonel Andrew Burr who led the troops of Connecticut Colony when Louisburg was captured. The old martial spirit had been kept alive through all the

years. Training days were still the lively and
delightful "outings" for the male population.

Sillabub continued a popular drink. One
old recipe said: "Fill your Sillabub Pot with
Syder, and good store of Sugar and a little
Nutmeg, stir it wel together, put in as much
thick Cream by two or three spoonfuls at a
time, as hard as you can as though you milke it
in, then stir it together exceeding softly once
about and let it stand two hours at least."
We cannot say positively that this was the
recipe followed always, but it was a favorite
mixture and served its purposes on many a
training day.

When the call came for men to serve
against Louisburg and Ticonderoga, Fairfield
responded generously; and when the successful campaigns were ended, the people of
the town again settled down to the common
business of the times.

Judge Peter Burr had passed to his reward
in 1724. Teacher, lawyer, auditor, deputy in
the town, speaker of the House, councillor

on the French and Indian war, judge of the County Court, chief judge of the Superior Court, he made a deep impression upon the life of Fairfield and the colony. But kindred spirits followed in his footsteps, and carried along the work which he and his predecessors transmitted to them.

It seemed a peaceable period for the town now that Indians and Frenchmen were settled, and there was little thought that the day drew on apace when the great conflict of the age was to be suddenly projected upon them.

Thaddeus Burr had graduated from Yale in 1755, and Jonathan Sturges four years later. They had entered upon the practice of law here in town. When the great questions of taxation were broached in the colonies, excitement and discussion prevailed in this provincial capital. The old lawyers and the young, business men and farmers, the pastor of the Prime Ancient Society and the keeper of the popular inn—they were all alive with the spirit of resistance.

VII.
War, Love, Captivity.

VII.

WE have reached the period when excitement ran so high that speech upon the street
was occasionally intemperate and vehement
beyond the limits set by the law of the land
and the authority of the Church; although the
conditions were such that strong and intense
forms of speech might be justified, if ever, on
the grounds of passionate loyalty to justice.

There is recorded the following illustration
of Church oversight, November 30, 1765. The
communication is addressed by Judge Eben-
ezer Silliman to Rev. Noah Hobart, pastor of
the First Church.

"Since my return home I am informed that
you have notified the communicants that the

sacrament of the Lord's Supper is to be administered the next Sabbath. You, I suppose, are not altogether unacquainted with the late public conduct of Job Bartram, one of the communicants of the church, which not only is offensive to me but many others of the church ; viz., in calling upon God to damn all that had any hand in making the Act of Parliament called the Stamp Act, and in libelling in the most ignominious manner some in the most elevated stations in civil authority ; which appears to me to be plain breaches of the third and fifth commands in the Moral Law, and inconsistent with the Christian character, the consideration whereof I recommend to you and the brethren of the church in the first society in Fairfield. I am with much consideration,

> "Your affectionate brother,
>   " E. SILLIMAN."

There was more or less correspondence upon this matter of rash and impulsive speech, and the trouble was finally settled to the common satisfaction ; Job Bartram working off his passion of loyalty, when occasion came, in bold defence of colonial liberties and Fairfield citizens.

That the good people of this town were particular in this matter of correct speech, is evident from some of the wills on record. One pious citizen, in devising certain property near what is called Devil's Den, does not venture to spell the profane word, but writes a capital *D*, then a dash, then a final *l ;* although another case, which might be construed to the contrary of this testimony, is also found in a certain will, where the good citizen leaves to one of his heirs his "damn."

Speaking of wills, some of their peculiar phrases are recalled. One man refers to himself as "crazy in body and merry in mind." Another man begins his will with the statement that he is "tender in disposition and weakness of body, but, thanks be to God, of a disposing mind and memory and of as Compos Mentis as ever I was."

7

The subject of wills suggests the extravagance of funeral occasions. To-day we even
go so far as to form societies for the purpose
of doing honor to the dead in better taste and
at less expense. But there is something to
comfort us when we read the narrative of these
occasions a century or two ago.

At one of the Winthrops' funerals, sixty
rings at a pound apiece were given away.
There were also scutcheons, hatchments, scarfs,
gloves, bell-tolling, clothes, and other necessary
expenses, amounting to three thousand dollars
—a third of the estate.

How curious this sounds : " It being artillery
day and Mr. Higginson dead, I put on my
mourning rapier, and put a mourning ribbon in
my little cane." The rings had such mottoes
as these : " Death parts united hearts ;" " Prepared be to follow me." How cheerful a man
must feel to carry several articles of such jewelry about with him !

The liquor consumed on these occasions
made no small item in the bill of expense.

Like ordinations, it was a time when the good people of the town sought relief for their emotional nature in copious draughts of their favorite beverage. No wonder that such extravagance and such customs became matters for public condemnation and discipline.

But a subtle change was passing over the face of common life. It was ferment and agitation all through the century. The character of discussion had been theological and ecclesiastical rather than political, although politics was an element in all the ferment. We have slight conception of the intense, bitter feelings engendered here and in neighboring places on account of religious differences. And yet our own observation teaches us that such differences are apt to lead to all sorts of conflict and persecution. But the time had now come when opinions and practices in respect to Christian faith were to yield precedence unto questions concerning colonial liberty and national life.

The Rev. Andrew Eliot had been invited to settle here as pastor of the Prime Ancient

Society after the death of Mr. Hobart. This promising young minister was the son of the famous man of the same name, pastor of the New North Church of Boston.

Dr. Eliot had been elected president of Harvard College, although he declined the honor, choosing to remain in the pastorate. He was the popular minister of his city, judging from the many public services which he performed. He kept a record of the gloves and rings which he received at funerals. During his pastorate he made a list of two thousand nine hundred and forty pairs of gloves.

Doubtless, young Andrew was well stocked with gloves when he came to Fairfield, and, if there continued any need, his father would supply him, although there were ten other children to draw on this stock. Dr. Eliot did not allow the gloves to go to waste, however; for he tells us that through the kindness of Boston milliners he sold what he did not use, and such sale brought him in the snug sum of nearly seven hundred dollars.

The new minister brought to Fairfield the fresh life of Cambridge and Boston. He was full to overflowing with generous and noble sentiments; and his patriotism found congenial company in the galaxy of educated lawyers and business men resident in Fairfield.

It was only a few months after his coming that these people sent to the suffering patriots of Boston a present of seven hundred and fifty bushels of grain. The letter of acknowledgment is worth remembering:

"Gentlemen: The testimony which the patriotic citizens of Fairfield have given of their attendance to the common and glorious cause of liberty . . . has afforded much comfort as well as seasonable relief to their friends in Boston, who are now suffering under the cruel rod of ministerial Tyranny and Oppression. . . . We are particularly obliged by the assurances which you give us that you are not insensible of our sufferings, and the hope that you express that you shall yet consider yourselves bound to afford us such succour and relief as your circumstances and our wants may demand. . . . May a kind Providence bountifully reward your liberality and kindness, and the blessings of Him that was ready to perish come down and rest on the heads of the generous inhabitants of the Town of Fairfield."

The patriotism of the people here had already taken a tangible form. On December 29, 1774, this same year, "at a legal meeting of the inhabitants," the action of the recent Continental Congress was discussed. It was approved, and the town took the opportunity "to express their most grateful sense of the good services of the worthy delegates from this colony who attended said Congress." There follow the names of a committee to act in conformity with the suggestions made by the Continental Congress.

It was also voted expedient to call a county congress to consider these matters of state, and it was voted that "Col. Gold S. Silliman, Jonathan Sturges, Andrew Rowland, Esq., Mr. Job Bartram, and Thaddeus Burr be a committee to attend at such time and place as they shall appoint." These gentlemen were also constituted a committee of correspondence for the town.

The announcement of hostilities between the British and the Continental forces came to Fairfield in a dramatic way. It was on an April morning.

Gold Selleck Silliman and Jonathan Sturges had come over to the house of Thaddeus Burr to discuss war prospects. They were all members of the town committee of war.

As they stood upon the porch of the great mansion earnestly engaged in conversation, a horseman dashed down the street and came to a sudden standstill just in front of them. He carried a sealed packet, which he hastily thrust into the hands of Mr. Silliman. Breaking the seal and glancing at the contents, more or less of the citizens having gathered meanwhile, General Silliman read aloud the following letter :

" To All Friends of American Liberty : Be it
known that this morning before break of day a
brigade consisting of about one thousand or
two thousand men landed at Phipps's farm,
Cambridge, and marched to Lexington, where
they found a company of our colony militia in
arms, upon whom they fired without provoca-
tion, and killed six men and wounded four
others. By an express from Boston we find
another brigade are on the march from Boston,
supposed to be about one thousand. The
bearer, Trail Bissell, is charged to alarm the
country quite to Connecticut, and all persons
are desired to furnish him with fresh horses as
they may be needed. I have spoken with several who have seen the dead and the wounded.

"J. PALMER,

" One of the Committee of S'y."

That sealed packet sounded a mighty bugle
call. It did not take long for the news to
spread, and ere it was the close of day, nearly
one hundred members of the train-band set

forth on a march to Boston. What emotions swelled within their breasts as they made their way along by the Green, the meeting-house, the home of the new minister!

As they cross Gould's bridge we see Colonel Abram Gould step forth to cheer them; and as he stands facing the marshes this earnest company passes on to share the conflict.

These were lively times. It was quite uncertain what turn events might take, but the feeling and purpose was common among our people to the end that they must stand by their rights and resist all encroachments upon their liberties.

There was a small party in opposition that continued in the town. It was natural that Mr. Sayre, the Episcopal minister, and the company of royalists that gathered about him, should show little sympathy with these aggressive movements. Politics and religion were one for the time being, since the Church of England must necessarily stand for the authority of the mother country.

As a consequence, there was considerable bitterness manifest toward certain individuals and families in town because their sympathies were naturally royalist in character. In one way or another these people were compelled to suffer humiliation. Many of them were finally driven from the town, and their property confiscated. Old friendships were broken, and family ties severed on more than one occasion, but this was the inevitable result of circumstances.

When the Articles of Association formed by the Continental Congress were presented to Mr. Sayre, rector of Trinity, he refused to sign them. Therefore he was banished from the town. After seven months of exile he was recalled, and permission was given him to stay within the limits of four miles, and later within the limits of the county. But he and the rest of the Episcopal brethren were forbidden the use of the liturgy in service.

Many of the Church of England parishes omitted public worship during this period of prohibition, but Mr. Sayre continued to hold some kind of public worship throughout the whole period. The reading of Scripture, the singing of hymns, repetition of Psalms and the Lord's Prayer, an extempore supplication, and a sermon, these did quite well for a service, and a worshipper might have thought that he had gotten into the place where the Prime Ancient Society was holding service, rather than the dissenting brethren of the Church of England.

A phrase which denotes the purpose of these faithful people to continue their worship under the most trying circumstances leads one to think that there might have been a certain cheerful freedom and unhampered expansiveness about it. We read, for example, that they voted " to carry on " in the room of Mr. Shelton. Did we give a present-day meaning to the phrase, we might look for something lively and festive in character. There are several votes of this kind. Trinity Church " carried on " for several years in one place and

another, until the time of rebuilding a sanctuary came to them and they were once more
safely housed on Mill Plain.

Meanwhile people lived at high tension, in
perpetual state of expectancy. Soldiers were
drilled in Fairfield and sent forth under various
commands to answer pressing needs. The
mansion of Thaddeus Burr was a centre of
social life in the town, and many were the society events which occurred within its ample
proportions. The Burrs were intimate with
several Boston families, and the new minister
also drew his friends down into the country
for various visits.

While the British occupied Boston, several
Bostonians took the opportunity to see their
Fairfield friends. Among them were Mrs.
Thomas Hancock, aunt of John Hancock, and
Miss Dorothy Quincy, daughter of Edmund
Quincy. Miss Quincy was engaged to Mr.
John Hancock, and they wanted to get mar-
ried. But the times were troublous: Boston
was beleaguered. A bird in the hand is

worth two in the bush. And the report came
to Mr. Hancock that Aaron Burr, son of the late
president of Princeton College, cousin of Miss
Quincy's host Thaddeus, was making himself
very agreeable to his *fiancée*. This attractive
gentleman was intimate with Thaddeus Burr.

It was quite natural that young Aaron should
share in the entertainment of the Boston
beauty. Fortunately for President Hancock,
Aaron Burr left Fairfield the summer of 1775
and sought renown and promotion in the cam-
paign against Canada, serving under Benedict
Arnold with Henry Dearborn (later the General
Dearborn of Chicago fame). The Rev. Samuel
Spring, father of Dr. Gardiner Spring, of New
York, was chaplain of the regiment, but according to tradition his ministrations did not keep
young Burr altogether straight.

During this period arrangements for the
marriage of Mr. Hancock and Miss Quincy were
made, and Mr. and Mrs. Burr entered heartily
into all the plans. When September came the
president of the Continental Congress gathered

various friends about him and left Philadelphia
for Fairfield.

The bridegroom was one of the wealthiest
men of New England. His station was exalted,
and the approaching marriage excited not a
little interest.

We are told that it was quite an imposing
cavalcade which came to town as escort to the
happy man. Those were the days when, in
spite of war, not a little pomp and circumstance
might be commanded in case of necessity.

It must have been an interesting sight.
Probably the boys and the girls, and perhaps
some of the grown folks in the town walked up
and down the streets and watched closely the
assembling company. The great massive coach
with liveried driver and footman, the attendant
cavaliers with gay uniforms and high-spirited
animals, the elegant and elaborate costumes of
the ladies, the mingling of old-time civil and
military display, all the accompanying excitement, activity, social cheer in liquid abundance,
and good-fellowship of heart and hand—what

an occasion it was, and how we should like to have been there!

But it was a day all too brief and fleeting for the merry onlookers. The old church record compresses the whole thing into one sentence:

"September 28, 1775. Married at the residence of Thaddeus Burr, Esq., by the Rev. Andrew Eliot, the Hon. John Hancock, President of the Continental Congress, to Miss Dorothy Quincy, daughter of Edmund Quincy, of Boston."

The honeymoon was occasionally interrupted by the cry of "British." A price had been put upon the head of Hancock, and he thought it expedient to keep quiet. Some of the time their meals were served in the privacy of the chamber.

We are told that one day when Mr. and Mrs. Hancock attempted to dine in state with the host and hostess, the dinner was hastily abandoned and the feast was lost on account of an alarm and supposed pursuit of the enemy. But with all these storm-clouds shifting across

the summer sky of their honeymoon, we may
rest assured that the Hon. John and Madame
Dorothy drank deep draughts of connubial bliss,
and gave grave care a thoughtless go-by for
the time being.

Among the favorite resorts of Fairfield society at this time was the Silliman home on
Holland Heights.   The location itself was such
that it attracted visitors.

Fairfield reposed securely to the right of the
eminence, and offered perpetual suggestion of
prosperity and affluence.   To the left was the
little hamlet which the years would transform
into the busy, energetic city of Bridgeport.
Grover's Hill was like an advance guard, keeping constant watch upon the sea.

" A situation perfectly rural," writes Professor Silliman, " on elevated ground overlooking
the country for many leagues ; having before
us Long Island Sound, a beautiful strait perhaps twenty miles in average breadth, a strait
often adorned by the white canvas of sailing-
vessels, occasionally fretted by winds and

storms into waves which adorned the blue
bosom of the deep with snowy crests and
ridges—in such a situation we had only to open
our eyes in a clear atmosphere to be charmed
with the scenery of this beautiful world. . . .
And with it were associated all the attractions
of the farm, of the forests and the waters, the
beauty and melody of birds, and the activity
and instinct of animals."

This was the home of General Gold Selleck
Silliman, a leading man in Fairfield and Connecticut at this period. He was prosecuting
attorney for the county at the time when the
Revolutionary ferment manifested itself. Becoming interested in military affairs, he was
made colonel of cavalry in the local militia and
took part in several battles.

We are indebted to the journal kept by Mrs.
Silliman for much valuable and interesting
information concerning the events of her day.
The piety of this noble woman is manifest on
many pages.

" Who among the human race," she writes on

8

one occasion, "has greater reason to be thank-
ful than I have this day? My dear husband
has been at home and made me a short visit;
but although I thought not a ball had touched
his clothes, afterward there was one found in
his coat pocket, the coat he had on the day of
the battle of White Plains. I took his coat to
mend it and found it. He supposes it was a
spent ball, and as his coat flew open it dropped
in. The ball was made ragged that it might
not be easily extracted from the flesh of him
who was so unhappy as to receive it."

General Silliman was active in the service of
the colony all through the trying days of organization. A devout man, deacon in the parish
church, appointed to all sorts of local tasks,
engaged in the practice of the legal profession
(it is pleasant to note that many of the officers
and leaders in the Prime Ancient Society have
been eminent and honored members of the bar),
General Silliman would naturally be a marked
man in the estimation of the British.

Fairfield itself was a conspicuous object for

the hatred of the enemy. The town stood seventh among the towns of Connecticut in taxable wealth. So far as social prestige, legal reputation, intellectual vitality, ecclesiastical fame, were concerned, it stood among the first towns of New England. The part which it took in the struggle for independence was conspicuous.

It had been voted on October 31, 1776, " that there be a guard of thirty-two men to guard the Town nightly, and every night to be set in the following manner: Four to patrol from Saugatuck River to Cable's Mill, and four to patrol from said Mill to Sasco River, and four from Sasco River to Mill River, and four from Mill River to Pine Creek, and six to patrol from Pine Creek to Ash House Creek, and six to patrol in the town streets, and four at Strathfield. Voted, that each of the guard have three shillings a night for their service. Voted, the guard be taken out of the Prime Society, Green's Farms, Greenfield, and Strathfield." In 1778 a guard of forty-two men was enlisted.

The alarm post here in town was the rallying place of the militia. The alarm list and the muster roll had long been prepared.

Although war was in the air, and on the soil for that matter, yet there was not a little business that demanded attention apart from the conflict with British authority. At one time it was voted that "Liberty for all be granted, and every person or persons to turn any flock or flocks of sheep on the highways within this town with a keeper of more than fifty to eat up and consume the herbage in and upon said highway."

It was this custom of appointing keepers to look after the flocks, to which the merchant Mr. Jonathan Sturges refers, in his address when the New York Chamber of Commerce honored him with a complimentary dinner.

" One of the first lessons I received was when eleven years of age," he remarked. " My grandfather had collected a fine flock of merino sheep." (The grandfather was Judge Jonathan Sturges, whose name was signed to the letter

sent to Boston in 1776.) "I was a shepherd boy.
. . . A boy who was more fond of his books
than of the sheep was sent with me, but left
the work to me while he lay in the shade and
read his books. I finally complained to the
old gentleman. I shall never forget his benig-
nant smile as he replied : ' Never mind; if you
watch the sheep, you will have the sheep.'"
This incident binds us to the life which we are
etching, the life of one hundred years and
more ago.

The time having come for soldier service, it
was voted by the town that "the proportion
of soldiers to be furnished in this Town for
the Continental service be made out according
to the Alarm List and Muster Roll of said
Society."

The Council of Safety of Connecticut voted,
on March 25, 1777, "to deliver to Selectmen of
Fairfield one six-pound and one three-pound
cannon." It seems a limited equipment, does
it not? The whole matter of defence was
necessarily put upon a meagre footing.

We know that the British felt they would soon settle the rebellious rabble, and teach us a lesson we never could forget. And such had been the result were it not that the Almighty had larger purposes in mind.

In 1779 General Silliman was stationed to guard the coast in the vicinity of Fairfield. Appeals had been made for help of this kind since the exposed position of the town signified grave peril. The command of General Silliman extended to the various outposts in the county, but he made his headquarters for the time being on Holland Heights.

On May 1, General Clinton, commanding officer at New York, sent a whaleboat and eight men to Fairfield in order to capture General Silliman. Mrs. Silliman, in her journal, continues: "At a midnight hour, when we were all asleep, the house was attacked. I was awakened by his calling out, 'Who's there?'

"At that instant there was a banging at both doors, they intending to break them down

or burst them open; and this was done with
great stones as big as they could lift. My
dear companion then sprang up, caught his
gun, and ran to the front of the house, and, as
the moon shone, saw them through the window, and attempted to fire; but his gun only
flashed in the pan and missed fire.

"At that instant they burst in a window, sash
and all, jumped in and seized him, and said he
was their prisoner and he must go with them.
He asked if he might dress himself. They
said 'yes,' if he would be quick.

"All this time I lay quaking. They followed
him into the bedroom where I and my dear
little boy were. With their guns and bayonets fixed, their appearance was dreadful. It
was then their prisoner addressed them in mild
terms and begged them to leave the room,
and told them their being there would frighten
his wife. They then withdrew for a minute or
two, and then returned, when he asked them
out again. They hurrying him, he went out
and shut the door. After that I heard them

breaking the windows, which they wantonly did with the breeches of their guns."

These soldiers then asked him for money, private papers, and other things. Mrs. Silliman writes : " He told them mildly he hoped he was in the hands of gentlemen, and that it was beneath them to plunder." This seems to have had an effect, although the men took a few things that came conveniently to hand. The communion silver, which is still used by the church, was deftly concealed, as were also certain valuable papers.

After the soldiers had gone, having taken both the general and his elder son, an alarm was given. But it availed naught. " I heard nothing from them in three weeks," says Mrs. Silliman. " My next step was to look for an asylum in case of an invasion of the town," she continues. The asylum was found with a friend in North Stratford. Here, some three months later, her son Benjamin, the famous and revered professor of natural science, was born.

General Silliman and his son were transported to Long Island and afterwards to New
York. It was a year before the exchange of
prisoners was made which set him free to return unto his station. Colonel Abram Gold,
the faithful and splendid soldier, had yielded
his life two years previous to this period. The
battle-ground of Ridgefield was stained with
his blood, although his body had been brought
in upright position upon his horse all the way
from the scene of death to his beloved town.

One noble patriot after another had given
himself and his property to the cause. General
Abel, whose home preceded the Benson house,
was serving the people with distinction. A
full quota of Fairfield men was distributed
through the various divisions of troops, so that
Fairfield was placed in a critical position. The
people besought the governor and council to
send an armed vessel to assist in guarding the
coast. But the vessel was not forthcoming,
and the town was compelled to shift for itself.

VIII.

The Burning of Fairfield.

VIII.

THE BURNING OF FAIRFIELD.

GENERAL TRYON had been a visitor here in Fairfield on several occasions, and a courteous hospitality made him welcome. But when he began warlike inroads among the shore towns, bitter feeling against him became widespread. Several thriving villages suffered under his pestilential touch. Fear possessed the people of this place that he meant ill to them.

When it became known that a small fleet of hostile ships was making its way along the Sound, the townsmen felt that the long-dreaded day was upon them. It is not difficult for us to picture the scene.

Fairfield was now one hundred and forty years old. Evidences of refinement and prosperity were scattered all through the place.

The streets were not as broad as they are to-
day; but trees shaded the walks, commodious
houses were distributed through ample yards,
the Green was a pleasant spot framed by public
and private buildings, trade flourished in the
town, and the leaders of thought, enterprise,
politics, lived in hospitable way, entertaining
many guests.

On Sunday, July 4th, when Mr. Eliot preached
his last sermon in the prim, angular, stately
meeting-house, the calm and beauty of the day
came like the suggestive quiet which precedes
the bursting of the tempest. It was not alone
that Fairfield was unprotected at this time;
but it was also that many of her soldiers were
absent in the service. To be sure, the coast
guard was doing its duty, and there was a cannon or two mounted on Grover's Hill. But
what were such resources in face of two large
men-of-war, forty-eight row galleys, tenders, and
transports? This was the fleet coming along
the shore toward the patriotic town.

It was Sunday night when the British passed

East view of the Court House, Church and Jail, Fairfield.

1776.

From an old print.

Fairfield. Monday and Tuesday they carried
on their business of desolation at New Haven.
The people here were alert and watchful. It
was a nervous, intense life which throbbed
along these familiar streets that week. Citizens
did not want to leave their homes. There was
a lingering hope that the place might be spared.
And yet their better judgment told them that
Fairfield was condemned to the ravishment of
the foe.

Had not the town done everything in her
power to advance the interests of independence? Money, supplies, soldiers, had they not
all been given with unstinted generosity? Did
not generals, judges, statesmen, leaders, make
Fairfield their home, and gather about them the
chief rebels and conspirators against the authority of the mother country? It was a very
hotbed of resistance, machination, patriotism,
liberty. It was not a fear of wolves, not a dread
of witches, not a terror of Indians, that possessed citizens ; but something quite as real and
awful. The thought that their streets might

be invaded by bitter enemies, their families in-
sulted and harassed by foreign hirelings, their
homes plundered and destroyed by heartless
and cruel men—this it was which caused them
to pass sleepless nights and restless days while
awaiting helplessly the pleasure of their foe.

The British sailed from New Haven on July
6th. All day long, men, women, and children
had walked the town, tarried down by the
shore, climbed the places where better views of
the Sound might be obtained, spent the hot,
anxious hours in a fever of alternate hope
and despair. The few soldiers that gathered
for the defence of the place were scattered
along the stretch of territory or massed in the
fort on Grover's Hill. This latter place had a
force of twenty-three men under command of
Lieutenant Isaac Jarvis.

The night of the 6th was spent in making
such further preparations as were necessary and
possible. The very children found it hard to
get sleep, for they had become infected with the
consuming patriotism of their parents.

The early morning came, and people began
to breathe with that freedom which follows the
darkness and suspense of the night.   Suddenly
the boom of a cannon carried its startling mes-
sage to the worn, brave watchers.   It was four
o'clock in the morning of the 7th.   The shot
had been fired at the British fleet, which just
came into sight.   It told the foe that we were
not a defenceless community.   For a time it
appeared that this bold, rash shot might have
changed the plan of the enemy, for they did
not stop.   Perhaps Fairfield was to escape, after
all.   At seven o'clock the fleet was moving
towards New York.   And then a dense fog
settled down upon the scene.

Thus ends act the first in this drama.

Two or three hours later the fog lifted.   The
fleet was close to shore.   Little Sam Rowland
was watching the course of events from the
spire of Trinity Church (which stood on land
now belonging to the Rowland homestead).
When it became evident that the enemy meant
assault, he hastily descended from his lofty

9

perch, jumped astride the old white mare, ran
along the main street, turned the corner by the
meeting-house, passed the home of Mr. Isaac
Jennings, and concealed himself in the woods,
where he kept an eye upon the struggle and
havoc for many hours, returning at last to his
home, which had been spared from the flames
on account of the tact and bravery of his
mother, Elizabeth Rowland, the daughter of
Governor Fitch.

"The boats being not sufficient for the whole
of the first division," says General Tryon in his
report to Sir Henry Clinton, "I landed only
with the flank companies of the Guards, one
company of the Landgrave's, and the King's
American Regiment, with two field-pieces,
east of the village and southwest of the Black
Rock battery which commands the harbor.
We pursued our march (under a cannonade
without effect) towards the village, but in our
approach received a smart fire of musketry.
The rebels fled before the rapid advance of the
Guards, and left us in possession of it, and of

the heights in the west, until General Garth,
who landed two miles in the south, joined us
with the remainder of the troops, in the evening."

The landing of the enemy was therefore
made in two divisions, according to the official
documents preserved in the war office of the
Government.   It was four o'clock in the afternoon before the troops landed.   The division
under Garth came by way of Sasco Hill.   The
division under Tryon came through Beach Lane
and made their way to the Green.

They were exposed to the cannon from
Grover's Hill; Samuel Squiers, Israel Chapman,
and Aaron Turney manning the small battery.
As they drew nigh the Green, such militia and
recruits as could be gathered made a stand
against the enemy's approach, from the vantage
point of the Court House.   One field-piece did
excellent service.   It threw the foe into considerable disorder, and obstructed the advance
for a brief time.   But it was simply a temporary delay.   The citizens felt all the time that

the British had them at their mercy and could do with them much as they pleased.

Mrs. Silliman heard the premonitory shots as she watched the action of the fleet from her view point on Holland Heights. She saw the enemy disembark, and she well knew that it meant common desolation. The general was still held a prisoner in New York.

"From the roof of our house," she writes, "we saw the enemy land, and I thought best to leave my habitation, having before made preparations for ordering up the team and loading it with some of our valuable effects. By this time the cannon began to roar, which pleased Selleck [the little boy], and he would mimic them, saying, 'Bang, bang!' but they were doleful sounds in our ears. The firing was heavier as we went on."

The curtain falls upon the second act.

Late in life Professor Silliman, referring to the severe experience of his mother at this time, wrote: "My mother's cheerful courage contributed to sustain her."

In her journal Mrs. Silliman, continuing her
account, exclaims: "Oh the horrors of that
dreadful night! At the distance of seven miles
we could see the light of the devouring flames
by which the town was laid in ashes. It was a
sleepless night of doubtful expectations. I returned to visit our house"—this was after the
withdrawal of the enemy—"and found it full
of distressed people whose houses had been
burned, and our friend Captain Bartram lay
there a wounded man."

Meanwhile many of the inhabitants were
doing just as Mrs. Silliman did, hastening back
upon the hills and into the remote districts in
order to find a place of security. It was infinitely sad and distressing to leave home and
the beautiful old town. Never did Fairfield
seem more precious and enchanting than on
the 7th of July, 1779. And there were many
places where comfort, elegance, refinement,
opulence, were manifest.

Scarcely a thing could be removed. The
silver might be thrown into the well. Grain-

fields were luxuriant and convenient. Odd
pieces of choice furniture, and occasional heir-
looms of value, were cast into these secretive
patches. A few treasures were carried by
the women and children in their flight. But
the great mass of household stuffs and
family possessions was left in the deserted
houses.

There were a few women that braved the foe
and remained to protect their property; but
they were cruelly treated, and barely escaped
the most frightful abuses. Andrew Eliot, in a
letter to his brother, gives a vivid account of
the events. "The Hessians were first let loose
for rapine and plunder. They entered houses,
attacked the person of Whigs and Tories indiscriminately; breaking open desks, trunks,
closets, and taking away everything of value.
They robbed women of their buckles, rings,
bonnets, aprons, and handkerchiefs. . . . Looking-glasses, china, and all kinds of furniture
were soon dashed to pieces. Another party
that came on were the American refugees,

who, in revenge for their confiscated estates, carried on the same direful business."

Dr. Timothy Dwight, in his " Travels," tells us how Mrs. Thaddeus Burr (Mr. Burr̄ was high sheriff of the county at this time) tried to save her house. She "probably had never known what it was to be treated with disrespect, or even with inattention. She made a personal application to Governor Tryon, in terms which, from a lady of her respectability, could hardly have failed of a satisfactory answer from any person who claimed the title of gentleman. The answer which she received was, however, rude and brutal, and spoke the want not only of politeness and humanity, but even of vulgar civility. . . . An attempt was made in the meantime by some of the soldiery to rob her of a valuable watch, with rich furniture; for Governor Tryon refused to protect her, as well as to preserve the house. The watch had been already conveyed out of their reach."

Thus ends the third act of the drama.

The fourth comes on apace. The town had been condemned. The first house fired was that of Isaac Jennings. Mr. Sayre, the Church of England minister, had done what he could to prevent the conflagration, but it was all in vain. The promise that his own home, the house of Andrew Eliot, and some other places might be saved had been wrung from the destroying Tryon; but the promise was broken.

Soon the home of General Abel was in flames. Then fire was seen in one and another place along the main street. And now the night settled down upon the doomed town.

What words can paint the sombre, lurid, frightful scene? Intermittent sounds of guns; loud and profane shouting of heartless men; occasional shrieks of unprotected women; boisterous revelling of plunderers fresh from the cider barrel and the wine cellar; crash of falling timbers and riot of angry flames as one after another structure is caught and held by the contagion of fire; men separated from wives and children; women driven forth into

the gloom and horror of the surrounding hills
and woods; children searching for parents, and
wild with fear and terror; distress, suffering,
hunger, sleeplessness, anxiety, sickness, misery,
on every side.

It was while this tumult raged through Fairfield that a storm added its sublime contribution to the general woe.

"The sky was speedily hung with the deep-
est darkness, wherever the clouds were not
tinged by the melancholy lustre of the flames."
The words of President Dwight are quoted.
"At intervals, the lightnings blazed with a
livid and terrible splendor. The thunder rolled
above. Beneath the roaring of the fires filled
up the intervals with a deep and hollow sound,
which seemed to be the protracted murmur of
the thunder, reverberated from one end of the
heaven to the other. Add to this convulsion
of the elements, and these dreadful effects of
vindictive and wanton devastation, the trem-
bling of the earth, the sharp sound of musketry occasionally discharged, the groans here

and there of the wounded and dying, and the shouts of triumph; then place before your eyes crowds of the miserable sufferers, mingled with bodies of the militia, from the neighboring hills taking a farewell prospect of their property and their dwellings, their happiness and their hopes, and you will form a just but imperfect picture of the burning of Fairfield."

Such was the night. "At sunrise," says Mr. Eliot, "some considerable part of the town was standing, but in about two hours the flames became general. . . . All the town from the bridge by Colonel Gould's to the Mill River, a few houses excepted, was a heap of ruins." The British withdrew to their ships about eight o'clock in the morning.

Thus ends the fourth act of the drama.

Standing on the spot and looking down upon the desolation, Colonel Humphrey wrote in 1779 his elegy on the "Burning of Fairfield":

"Ye smoking ruins, marks of hostile ire,
    Ye ashes warm, which drink the tears that flow,

Ye desolated plains, my voice inspire,
  And give soft music to the song of woe.
How pleasant, Fairfield, on the enraptured sight
  Rose thy tall spires and ope'd thy social halls !
How oft my bosom beat with pure delight
  At yonder spot where stand thy darkened walls !
But there the sound of mirth resounds no more ;
  A silent sadness through the streets prevails.
The distant main alone is heard to roar,
  And hollow chimneys hum with sudden gales,
Save where scorched elms th' untimely foliage shed,
  Which rustling hovers round the faded green ;
Save where at twilight mourners frequent tread,
  Mid recent graves, o'er desolation's scene.

.   .   .   .   .   .

"Tryon, behold thy sanguine flames aspire,
  Clouds tinged with dyes intolerably bright.
Behold well pleased the village wrapped in fire ;
  Let one wide ruin glut thy ravished sight.
Ere fades the grateful scene, indulge thine eye ;
  See age and sickness, tremulously slow,
Creep from the flames ; see babes in torture die,
  And mothers swoon in agonies of woe.
Go, gaze enraptured with the mother's tear,
  The infant's terror, and the captive's pain,

Where no bold bands can check thy curst career ;
Mix fire with blood on each unguarded plain.
These be thy triumphs ; this thy boasted fame.
Daughters of memory raise the deathless song.
Repeat through endless years his hated name,
Embalm his crimes, and teach the world our wrong."

A brief account of the "Burning" is given
in the Hartford *Courant* of the following
week. It speaks of a district two miles in extent wasted, only sixteen houses in the whole
section left standing, the most of these having
been set on fire and then extinguished.

One incident is related to illustrate the bar-
barity of the foe. "A Fairfield man in arms
with us," says the correspondent, "who two
years ago deserted from the king's troops,
after being wounded, surrendered and begged
for quarter, was after this cruelly pierced and
tortured with bayonets, still keeping life in
him, then wrapped in a linen sheet wet with
'oil,' which was barbarously set on fire, and
thus the unhappy victim perished in flames."

General Tryon briefly dismisses the whole

subject in these words: "Having laid under arms that night, and in the morning burned the greatest part of the village, to resent the fire of the rebels from their houses and to mask our retreat, we took boat where the second division had landed."

The fifth scene of the drama reveals the sorrow and misery of the desolated town. Think of the tragic conditions. The withdrawal of the enemy gave the scattered families opportunity to return. They brought with them the few things which they had taken away in the hasty departure before the town was burned.

As the people came down from Mill Hill, Round Hill, Osborn Hill, Holland Hill, there stretched before them clouds of smoke rising from the smouldering ruins. It was infinitely pitiful. Yonder stood the powder-house on the rise of ground now owned by Mr. Edward Osborn. Here and there through the rifts of enswathing smoke-cloud, the stained form of a solitary house was seen. A half dozen build-

ings perhaps remained standing. Mrs. Lucretia
Redfield stayed in charge of her home, and put
out the flames four times. (This noble woman
became the wife of Isaac Marquand.) Invent-
ive Mrs. Nichols found an original use for yarn
and the dye tub, by converting them into a
fire extinguisher, so that her home was saved.
Tryon made the Bulkley house his headquarters, and this was saved. Truth compels us to
say, however, that this comfortable mansion
came near a later destruction at the hands of
the returning loyal citizens, because the owners
were royalists.

What a picture presented itself to the harassed citizens of the town as they once more
walked its streets! Heaps upon heaps of
ashes ; charred remains of timbers, tree trunks,
implements of toil, means of conveyance;
yards, gardens, fields, stained and blackened by
ashes and half-burnt pieces of wood; broken
furniture, torn garments, remains of things
precious and beautiful, tossed about hither and
thither in wind and rain ; domestic animals

destroyed, injured, or affrighted ; provisions
gone, and small stock of food or clothing upon
which to draw in cases of necessity ; the forms
of several dead men (the body of a Hessian
was buried just by the side of the meeting-
house ruins).

"The distress of this poor people is inex-
pressible," writes Mr. Eliot.   There were some
two hundred and eighteen buildings destroyed
—the churches, court-house, jail, schoolhouses,
ninety-seven dwellings, sixty-seven barns, forty-
eight stores and shops.   Eighty families had
their taxes abated, by action of the General
Assembly, on account of their losses.

Twenty-two   days after the conflagration,
Andrew Eliot gathered his congregation upon
the Green in front of the charred remains of
the meeting-house, and there delivered a memorable address.   That same sermon was preserved in the corner-stone of the later church
edifice.

The fifth sanctuary was burned on the night
of May 29 and the morning of May 30, 1890.

Who that was present in the Town Hall on the following Sunday, June 1st, can forget the moment in the service when the pastor held in his hand the old yellow manuscript of Mr. Eliot's sermon delivered on the Green one hundred and eleven years before? A quotation from the ancient address thrilled the congregation, and brought tears to many eyes.

We had just seen a flame compacted temple, walls fire studded, roof fire thatched, tower fire buttressed, fire columns holding aloft a palpitant pillar of fire. We had seen this luminous, flaming house of God caught up into the heavens and vanish from our sight. And as the words of Andrew Eliot sounded in our ears, it did seem for a moment that we were transported into the past, and made to share the grief, the poverty, the desolation, of the people who stood out under the blue sky in the midst of memorable ashes, and worshipped God in nature's sanctuary.

In his few words of personal statement Mr. Eliot stood forth as an example of many among his parishioners. "Not a house for my shelter, two-thirds of my personal estate plundered and consumed, a wife and three small children dependent on me for their maintenance. . . . I feel myself in a state of uncertainty as to many of the necessities of life. . . . And yet," he continued, "I am ready to undergo any difficulties in the work of the ministry for your sakes."

So this noble workman released his people from the burden of his salary until such time as they might be able to renew their care of him. He struggled along as best he could under the circumstances.

It is pleasant to record the fact that the New North Church in Boston remembered Mr. Eliot in his extremity, and took up a generous collection for him when the condition of affairs in Fairfield was known. So that another bond was formed between the two towns. The sermon was preached on the day of the collection by Dr. Simeon Howard, who took for his text the words, " It is more blessed to give than to receive."

10

So we drop the curtain upon this fifth act of the drama.

It was a new phase of life upon which the people of Fairfield now entered. Experience had taught them some rough lessons. We do not wonder that they refused to look upon the Tories with favor. The long list of confiscated estates found in the town records is just about what was to be expected under the circumstances. The people here were suddenly confronted with poverty. They had been accustomed to the comforts and even the luxuries of life. Prosperity had smiled upon them through well nigh every year of growth. Now they were homeless, foodless, almost without clothes.

But with all their deprivation and suffering they were far from hopeless. Mr. Eliot struck a responsive chord when he told them he was ready to undergo difficulties with them. Pinched and stricken as they were, a force of rebound and vitality was immediately manifest.

The people gathered what boards and timbers they could find and erected temporary quarters. Some of the families used old sheds that had escaped the fire. Thaddeus Burr fixed over a little shop. Later his good friend Governor Hancock supplied him with a part of the material for the rebuilding of his mansion on the old site, the simple condition of the gift being that Mr. Burr's house should be modelled after the mansion of Governor Hancock in Boston.

So there began to rise from the tell-tale ruins humble, modest dwellings, and such shops and stores as the times justified.

The town watchmaker recovered his wares from the chinks in the old well where he had concealed them. Pewter and silver were drawn up from the depths of their receptacles.

The elaborate clothes of Revolutionary days were forthcoming from some inexplicable source. A new Town Hall was built, where the Prime Ancient Society worshipped. Soldiers returned from their campaigns and settled down to business. The belief that the Colonies

were bound to win strengthened.   At last came
the day of peace.

In January, 1788, Mr. Thaddeus Burr and
Judge Jonathan Sturges were delegates to the
State convention at Hartford, called to ratify
the new Constitution.   When the first Congress
convened in New York, Judge Sturges represented Fairfield.   " The evening years of his
life," as Mr. Silliman tells us in his reminiscences, " were devoted to the bench of the
Supreme Court of the State of Connecticut."
" With a fine person," Mr. Silliman continues,
" Judge Sturges had the superior manners
of that day, dignity softened by a kind and
winning courtesy, with the stamp of benevo-
lence."

There was what might be called a re-organ-
ization of things in this old New England
town.   It was upon the footing of independence that life was now constructed.   There
was less of the show and pomp that cling to
monarchies.   People were compelled by circumstances to be modest in their display.

Government was conducted on a scheme of
simplicity that did not call for any great expen-
diture of money.

While the leaders gathered here in Fairfield
much as in days of yore, there was a certain
atmosphere of economy. The social activity
soon regained itself. The little companies
which came to the new home of Thaddeus Burr
and discussed with Dr. Timothy Dwight the
questions of religion, politics, and literature
fairly represented the prevailing tone of life in
the place. And one can find no more vivid,
interesting setting forth of social activity at
the time than that which is given us in the
home of this honored Thaddeus and Eunice
Dennie Burr. Let us picture it as the records
give us the precious details.

There stands the mansion, large, chaste, elegant, hospitable, surrounded by trees that had
escaped the ravages of the conflagration.
There are three stories to the edifice, and the
spaces are high between the floors. The dignity of pillars in front, sustaining the roof of

the antique porch contributes to the attractive-
ness of the structure.

One first enters the great hall of the mansion. Commodious rooms are on the right
hand and the left. Furniture has been sent
down from Boston, and many curious and
beautiful things adorn the generous interior.
There is an air of welcome which interprets the
spirit of master and mistress.

Mr. Burr was a man of fine presence, carrying with him all the old-time grace peculiar to
high life in the Colonies. But the informing
spirit of the home is Eunice Dennie the wife.

Copley made frequent visits here, so that we
know exactly how both Mr. and Mrs. Burr
looked. The portrait of Mrs. Burr was recently exhibited in the New York Academy
of Design. The figure is life size; the dress
characteristic of the times. The pose is
queenly. The reproduction of the face, which
is familiar to many of us, reveals rare beauty
and strength. Educated, refined, familiar
with the best society of the land, a natural

leader in the social realm, "adorned with all the qualities which give distinction to her sex, possessed of fine accomplishments and a dignity of character scarcely rivalled" (this last sentence is a tribute from Dr. Dwight), Mrs. Burr charmed every visitor and quickened every mind that came within the spell of her sweet and virtuous enchantment.

It was a distinguished succession of guests which rested in that memorable home. The great and the good of a generation turned often to its gracious privileges. It was not alone that John Hancock, Edmund Quincy, Samuel Adams, and other Boston or Massachusetts leaders came to visit Mr. and Mrs. Burr. Jefferson, Burr, Lafayette, Franklin, and the company of men that shaped the destinies of the Republic sought the repose and enjoyment of such society. Thaddeus Burr's sister had married Lyman Hall, one of the signers of the Declaration of Independence from Georgia. Dr. Dwight, referring to life in this home, speaks of "the elegant hospitality," "the refined enjoyments," "the works of charity," "the rational piety, which was at once the animating and controlling principle," so that it "diffused a brilliancy marked even by the passing eye." There were no children to brighten the days for Mr. and Mrs. Burr, but they gave themselves with regal generosity to their friends and the public. In the old house, Susan, the sister of .Colonel Aaron Burr, had been a constant visitor, and here it was that she was married to Judge Reeves, of Litchfield. But any attempt to paint the scenes and chronicle the doings that belong to the life of these people would prove futile.

The Burr homestead came into the possession of Gershom, a nephew of Mr. Thaddeus Burr. This Gershom married Priscilla Lothrop, step-daughter of Noah Hobart. They were the parents of General Gershom Burr, who inherited the property. General Burr married a daughter of Andrew Eliot. The historic place was sold in the early years of this century to Mr. Obadiah Jones.

Circumstances put Mrs. Burr and Mrs. Silliman to the forefront during this period of struggle and triumph. They were lovely and gifted women, fitted to adorn the most elevated station. The Daughters of the American Revolution have shown their wise, discriminating, appreciative reading of local history in naming two of their chapters after these eminent women. Their memory should be treasured with fadeless loyalty and affection.

But let it be distinctly understood that they stand forth as types of women that flourished during these tragic, eventful days. From the necessities of the case the men played the conspicuous parts. But it was the vital, inspiring patriotism of the mothers, the wives, the sisters, that made possible our national independence.

There were no tasks from which these brave, great women shrank. Did it come as the stern bidding of duty, they were prepared to handle the musket or fire the cannon. And yet withal there was a beautiful womanliness about them which perpetually witnessed to a native worth of mind and spirit that made them peers among the womankind of all ages.

So as we think of these Fairfield heroines cheerfully enduring privation, faithfully sustaining the men in their battle for liberty, submitting without murmur to the sorrows and terrors of war, infusing fresh enthusiasm into life when the tide seemed setting against them, retaining their noble ideals and illustrating their Christian graces through all the uncertainties and desolations of conflict, we are to think of them as precious and illuminating souls, noble in their lives, worthy our imitation and the unstinted reverence of all men.

IX.

Poverty, Education, Conflict.

IX.

REFERENCE has been made to the marriage of the Rev. Noah Hobart. Another interesting courtship culminating in wedlock is noted at the period under review. Andrew Eliot was son of the parish minister of the same name, grandson of Andrew Eliot, D.D., of the New North Church, Boston.

I have been told that recently a man applied to the town clerk for a license to marry, and when questioned as to the name and age of the supposed happy object of his affections, he replied with surprise that he had not yet settled upon a woman; he just thought he would get a license and carry it with him in case he did decide the matter.

Now, young Andrew Eliot was in love. It

was Saturday morning that he made up his
mind to marry. The object of his affections
was well known. So that very day he went to
the lady and asked her to become his wife on
the following evening. This seemed rather a
short time to make the trousseau, send out
wedding invitations, and prepare the marriage
feast. But Miss Sophia and her mother said
they would consider it through the day, and the
answer would be forthcoming in the evening.

As the mother was baking, she concluded
that it would make little additional trouble to
bake the wedding cake ; and as the daughter
found a presentable white dress among her
gowns, the way seemed clear for the union.
The next morning the banns were published
at church, and the happy couple were made one
in the evening. This Mr. Eliot was pastor of
the old church in New Milford.

This was doubtless a method peculiar to Mr.
Eliot ; but it is doubtful if many of the people
made elaborate preparations for these cere-
monies at this time. Susan, a sister of this

Andrew Eliot, married the Rev. Nathaniel Hewit, D.D. She was his second wife. Dr. Hewit's first wife, a daughter of Senator Hillhouse of New Haven, died early in their married life.

Although the parish church was rebuilt in 1786, it was seventeen years before the people were able to complete the woodwork, plastering, and glazing of the interior. It was forty-two years ere the edifice, painted inside and outside, was really finished. This is only one indication of the common poverty. Early in the century, sickness prevailed widely, and the people organized "The Charitable Society" in order to meet the needs of many sufferers. This was another indication of the needs peculiar to the town at this period.

The flag of our country has passed through various changes. In 1818 the Congress of the United States adopted a new design made by Captain S. C. Reid, a distinguished naval officer. It fell to the lot of Mrs. Reid to make the first flag in accordance with the new design. The

lady's name, with the names of those that as-
sisted her, was inscribed upon the flag. Mrs.
Reid was a Fairfield woman. It is pleasant
for us to remember that the daughter of Captain Nathan Jennings performed this patriotic
service for our country.

And this was quite in line with the services
of many another Fairfield woman whose work
has contributed to the history of our land.
What the good women of the town suffered
through the years that succeeded the Revolution was bravely concealed. Few were the
complaints heard. On every side retrenchment
and closest economy were essential.

At the time of the burning there were forty
or fifty stores and shops, that gave an air of
business to the place. A few of these were
rebuilt, but many of them had no successors.
Trade was gradually diverted to other towns.

It was during this period, when Fairfield
sought to recover her position, that Bridgeport
took its start. There had been a scattered life
manifest in Strathfield and Pequonnock, but

the county seat overshadowed such obscure activity. Now the current of enterprise flowed in the direction of what was termed New Field. The excellent harbor was reason enough for the development of this part of the town. And it was manifest ere long that Fairfield had a competitor for leadership close upon her borders.

As the years hastened it was evident that the scattered houses to the east, which the old citizens of this place considered as a sort of suburb to Fairfield, were rapidly becoming a prosperous village, outstripping the county seat itself. It was not many years before it was generally accepted that business would gravitate to Bridgeport, while Fairfield would be left to its honorable traditions and its historic associations.

There was neither envy nor regret on the part of either people. The residents of Fairfield with few exceptions desired their native place to retain in so far as it was possible its ancient, interesting character. They were re-

11

luctant to see the town given over to trade and manufacture.

The people of New Field, on the other hand, had already caught the spirit of industrial enterprise and commercial service. So the business that according to the nature of things would have centred in Fairfield was handed over to Bridgeport, or sought a larger sphere of operation in New York.

But while these changes were taking place, Fairfield continued to thrive in a certain quiet, conservative way, and throb with a life that was exceedingly fruitful. The days when cities were to multiply and take larger part in the history of the nation were coming on apace. The days when villages like Fairfield and Litchfield must take a quite subordinate position in the public records were already upon them.

Nevertheless the old leadership was not yielded without a struggle. If the men that shaped affairs were not as numerous here as during earlier days, it was found that many a leader reverted to Fairfield as the home of his ancestors.

The parents of Joel Barlow moved to Redding, but the family left traces of their importance in giving their name to that section of our town called Barlow's Plain. The poet and statesman himself was a frequent visitor. When he did his work for literature and the nation, it was felt that this old New England town had a part in it. When his untimely death in Poland occurred, there were sincere mourners in this place.

It is along these years that the name of Marquand appears in the church records, and the American ancestors of Frederick and Henry Marquand gathered that sterling manhood which they were to transmit unto their successors. The love of knowledge, education, music, art, which the sons of the present generation have manifested in their regal gifts to the public shows what kind of stuff they inherited from this Fairfield stock.

It is pleasant to recall such names and note

the part which these men and their descendants have taken in public affairs.   There was
Andrew Ward, an early settler of the place,
who was appointed one of the assistants or
judges in the first legislative body of the
colony, a man who finally chose Fairfield for
his home, and became one of the large property holders and one of the influential men of
his day.   His honorable descendants have
scattered all through the nation.   Among
them we name the Rev. Henry Ward Beecher.
The Society of Colonial Wars has another
member of the family for its secretary, a gentleman who has rendered most efficient and
valuable service to the encouragement of his-
torical research and commemoration.

For generations the Pells of New York and
Pelham have been distinguished for their leadership in various spheres of life.   Dr. Thomas
Pell, a London gentleman, was one of the first
settlers of Fairfield.   His estate passed to a
nephew, John Pell.   For some years this latter
gentleman continued his residence in this

place; but he at length purchased a large estate in East Chester, N. Y., and came with some ten Fairfield families to settle the virgin territory near the young city at the mouth of the Hudson. Mr. Pell was called "Lord of the Manor," and a part of the town was named Pelham Manor.

Education was always dear to the people of Fairfield, and many excellent and accomplished men served the public as school-teachers. A large proportion of the active citizens of the place were college graduates. The intellectual atmosphere stimulated the youth to study and professional life. The Fairfield men that have preached the gospel, practised law or medicine, become prominent educators, or taken a leading part in public affairs constitute a very large company.

But it was not until the beginning of this century that an academy flourished in the place. When the people had recovered from the Revolution, they set themselves to the task of organizing this higher institution of

learning.   The original trustees were Jonathan
Sturges, Andrew Eliot, David Judson, Nathan
Beers, Jr., and Samuel Rowland.

There are many famous names in the cata-
logue of instructors.   Professor Dutton, who
filled the chair of astronomy and mathematics
in Yale at a later date; Professor S. J. Hitch-
cock, afterward an instructor in Yale ; Rev. E.
W. Baldwin, D.D., president of Wabash College; Hon. Orrin Fowler, minister, orator,
reformer, member of Congress; Rev. G. E.
Pierce, D.D., president of Western Reserve
College; Hon. Henry Dutton, governor of
Connecticut and judge of the Superior Court;
Rev. Daniel March, D.D.; Mr. Henry Day, the
eminent jurist; Rev. William E. Moore, D.D.,
ex-moderator of the Presbyterian General Assembly; and other like men.

Such teachers were bound to impart more
or less enthusiasm to their pupils.   And it was
a congenial set of men with whom they were
brought into association.   The clergy made
Fairfield a favorite resort.   The courts still

drew the best legal talent of the country to the town. The old families connected with the leaders of thought, fashion, politics, theology, in New England, were always entertaining guests that contributed to the general fund of intellectual life.

There was great regret on the part of our townsmen when Timothy Dwight was elected president of Yale College, for it was felt that Fairfield as well as Greenfield Hill would lose one of her eminent citizens. Dr. Dwight was closely identified with the social, religious, and intellectual activity of the whole town. But when he sold his place to Dr. Isaac Bronson, the cultured and sagacious financier, it was felt that some one had come among the people that would help to fill the place vacated by Dr. Dwight.

Dr. Bronson's grasp of public affairs was national in its proportions. Long and serious were the conversations which he held with Judge Sherman when the public finances were in an appalling condition. And we are told

that it was one result of these wise, profound discussions on the part of Judge Sherman and Dr. Bronson that relief was suggested.

Many are the eminent people that received
some part of their education in the academy.
There were times when students came to the
school from the South and the West, as well as
from the East and the North. Among the
pupils were John C. Calhoun, Francis C.
Granger, afterward postmaster-general, and
other men equally notable and conspicuous.

On the top of the cupola to the building
there rests a curious and interesting ball, com-
posed of some sixty pieces. It was the gift
of Mr. Thomas F. Rowland, who built the
famous " Monitor."

No sooner were the difficulties with Great
Britain during the early part of this century
manifest, than Fairfield was again thrown into
a ferment of unrest and anxiety. The ships
of the British navy were familiar objects along
these shores, and it was felt that the Connecti-

cut towns on the Sound presented an attractive object for the mischief makers.

War was declared, and this State showed its bitter opposition. When the President called upon Connecticut to contribute militia for the prosecution of the war, there was misunderstanding and contention. These shores were left without protection. The State militia rallied to the support of local interests, but it was felt that such help was insufficient.

Then came the famous Hartford convention, in which Judge Sherman took a leading part. In fact, he was pronounced the great man of the occasion.

Widespread was the concern and dismay which prevailed through the war of 1812. The little fort at Black Rock was manned. The local militia again filled the streets with their music and their excitement. Yet it was apparent that the task were an easy one did the British wish to repeat their assault and again burn Fairfield to the ground. For months the anxiety and watchfulness pre-

vailed.   New London was threatened, and Mrs.
Jonathan Sturges tells in her "Reminiscences"
how her family buried their china in the garden,
and secreted other valuables as best they could,
thinking that the town would be destroyed.

One day a small fleet appeared off the
bar and then anchored in Bridgeport harbor.
Breastworks had been thrown up on Grover's
Hill.   An old twelve-pound cannon, mounted
on a pair of cartwheels, was brought forth and
placed upon the Green.   General Gershom
Burr was made commanding officer, and an
alarm was sounded about sundown.

Early in the evening men began to arrive,
and by daylight some two thousand citizen
soldiers were assembled on the beach.   But
the British ships had disappeared, and so the
troops dispersed.

The fort on Grover's Hill was constructed
of rocks covered with dirt and turf.   It was
garrisoned by Captain Hanford and about
thirty United States soldiers.   It was large
enough to hold one hundred men.

During this war the old powder-house was again brought into frequent service. The dangerous explosive was kept away from the centre of traffic and life ; and powder brought to town was always lodged in this little stone building.

When the house was first built, it was put under the charge of Thaddeus Burr, Esq.; for we read a vote of the General Assembly, taken during the first years of the Revolution, that Thaddeus Burr was "to take charge of all the powder sent to Fairfield."

One night during the war of 1812, a large wagon heavily laden with kegs or barrels was driven up to Knapp's tavern on the corner, the horses unhitched, and the men pleasantly housed in very comfortable quarters. Two of the academy boys, sons of an ex-governor, were curious to know the contents of said wagon. Taking an auger, therefore, they proceeded to bore a hole in one of the barrels, when the powder poured forth in a big stream, and the boys left the place in hot haste. An observer close at hand saw the transaction, gave the alarm, had the stuff transported to the powder-house on the hillside, and quite likely saved the town from a small earthquake.

It was only a generation since the nation had won its independence. Many citizens living at the time of this second war with Great Britain had shared the first struggle. But this second affair did not have the glory about it that marked the first. People were all the time wishing it to end. At last a settlement of difficulties was made and peace declared. Then the country went wild with thanksgiving.

One of the liveliest and most noteworthy celebrations was held here in Fairfield. The citizens appointed Friday, February 25th, as the day to celebrate. In the morning there was a Federal salute from Fort Union at Black Rock. This was answered by a salute fired by Colonel Burr's artillery located upon the Green. People flocked into the place from all the surrounding country. A great throng filled the streets and ignored the weather.

At ten o'clock the procession was formed at Fort Union. Citizens marched in large numbers, and they were followed by the State troops. Then appeared a very pretty sight. A long boat had been taken and beautifully decorated with the flags of many nations. This gay object was drawn by thirty picked youths.

"The day of the celebration," says Mr. Henry Rowland, in his graphic reminiscences of this period, "was stormy, a deep snow falling." George Rowland took a boat and put it on sleigh-runners with drag-ropes attached. About thirty youths manned this craft.

When the two gay and curious boats met in the street, the cry went forth from each of them, "Ship ahoy! Who are you? Where from? Whither bound? How many days out?" They were the sensation of the hour.

The martial music, the brilliant display of colors, the shining weapons of war, the happy companies of men and soldiers—it all made a pageant long remembered with keen delight by the thousands of on-lookers. Arrived at the parish church, as large a proportion of the throng as was possible passed into the edifice, and there joined in expressions of congratulation that the war was ended. Dr. Humphrey, the pastor of the old church, gave an eloquent and inspiring address. Then the procession was re-formed, and after some marching the citizens and the soldiers proceeded to test the quality of the great ox which had been roasted whole upon the Green for their benefit.

Tradition says that the men who got the first cuts fared better than those who came later. The meat grew very rare as the feast proceeded; and it was only on the second day that many of the revellers were able to find a piece done to their liking.

One account of the celebration says: " The ox was served up to rich and poor alike, and they enjoyed it together." But I suspect there was considerable imagination about the enjoyment of it, if the truth were known.

Meanwhile the ladies were having their feast in the second story of the court-house. Five hundred of them sat down together and had what the Hartford *Courant* calls " an elegant dinner."

At sunset another Federal salute was fired. When the darkness had set in, and people had prepared their candles, there was a universal illumination.   The amount of tallow consumed that night was simply appalling.   A necessary economy in light extending through months followed.

Dr. Humphrey was opposed on principle to such waste and extravagance.   So he left his house without light.   But Miss Mary Hobart did not intend that her pastor should be made conspicuous by darkness.   She took the matter in hand, and compelled the minister against his mind to fill his windows with the innumerable tallow dips, and shine his loyalty into the eyes of the shifting throngs upon the street.

Then when Sunday came Dr. Humphrey enjoyed a mild revenge by preaching from the text, " I will praise the name of God with a song, and will magnify Him with thanksgiving.

This also shall please the Lord better than an ox or bullock that hath horns and hoofs." So the good man not only showed his disapproval of the illumination, but also took occasion to "let fly" at the poor ox " barbecued " on the Green.

One feature of the illumination was a tall tree with cross sticks all the way from the ground to the tree-top, capped each by a tar barrel. This pyramid of light shone far into the night.

While this illumination was blazing away in all glory, men, women, and children perambulated the streets, and basked, so to speak, in the unnatural effulgence until about nine o'clock. The Washington Hotel was then the common object of interest. A splendid and brilliant ball gave a touch of elaborate finish to the festivities. Wealth, beauty, fashion, culture, power, they were all on hand to grace the occasion.

When it was ended, Fairfield felt that she had done the square thing for herself and the country in emphasizing the common jubilation. It is doubtful if Dr. Humphrey attended the ball, for he was frank to express his disapproval of that particular form of thanksgiving. But one of his predecessors was differently minded, which occasioned the characteristic remark by a parishioner, that "she certainly hoped her minister would be converted before he died."

12

X.

The Social Atmosphere.

X.

THE SOCIAL ATMOSPHERE.

MANY interesting details of life during the early part of the century are preserved in the journals of Miss Sarah White. This maiden lady was a very active member of society. Her notes extend through a period of fifty years. She was thoroughly versed in the affairs of the town, and her means of gathering information were characteristic.

It was an age when the tea-party was a favorite form of dissipation. The reading of Miss White's journal would convey the impression that Fairfield society was kept in a perfect whirl of tea-party gayeties. Cosey little visits where the company numbered two, the informal gathering of five or six friends, the conventional afternoon when all society was present, these were the popular varieties. "I took tea with Dr. Dodge [a brother of William E. Dodge] at Deacon Judson's," Miss White observes.

Occasionally the festive company came together at mid-day and enjoyed an orthodox New England dinner. Mrs. Dr. Hull was accustomed to give an annual noon feast to the widows of Fairfield. This led Miss Mary Hobart to do something in the same line, with a certain important difference. If the widows deserved such attention and enjoyment, she was' persuaded that the spinsters deserved something equally fine. So the maiden ladies of Fairfield were all invited to dine with Miss Hobart. Some wag rang the church bell at noon in honor of the unique company.

Turkey was only eight cents a pound at this time. It was the day of barter. "I bought a pint of gin and some raisins, and paid for them in eggs," writes the methodical Miss White. She gives us many a fresh view into the current of life.

Sunday night was the favorite wedding occasion. As the people all kept Saturday evening, the evening of the Lord's Day was something in the nature of holiday. It was not
considered a time to work, and yet the proper
number of hours had been devoted to rest and
worship. So there was a compromise, and the
evening was devoted to light tasks and social
activities.

Illumination was by means of candles. People made their own light, supplied themselves
with wood, did the family weaving at home,
raised a large portion of the produce consumed
in the house and on the place. It was, in fact,
the age of homespun.

Training day still continued an occasion of
frolic, although the great temperance move-
ment, which had been shared with such enthusiasm by Dr. Humphrey and Dr. Hewit,
had toned down the character of the fun and
frivolity. Aunt Dinah and Uncle Kit brought
their barrel of home-brewed beer on to the
meeting-house steps regularly each first Mon-

day of May and September. They sold their cards of gingerbread at two cents apiece, and election cakes at five. The boys and the girls watched the military display with the same intense interest that had marked their ancestors for five generations; and many a manly heart beat with new life when admiring maidens smiled their approval upon the favored hero.

Dancing and card-playing had been very popular during the latter part of the eighteenth century here in town. But popular amusements were again put under the ban by the leaders of society. The hours and the energies that had been devoted to the important matters of Church and State in earlier years were now given to the consideration of the small questions which have to do with neighborhood relations.

The community life was familiar. Anything that interested one person interested all. Personal and family affairs were everybody's business. This is one of the chief advantages of living in a small town. One can benefit by the watchfulness and criticism of his neighbors. Often friends will know more about a man's business than the man himself. They take an outside and disinterested view of the situation, as it were, and gratuitously help a man to do what he ought to do. City life has a tendency to destroy this mutual oversight and fraternal coöperation.

One of the features of Miss White's journal is the concise way in which she refers to this frequent duty and privilege of neighborhood watch-care. They met at Mrs. A's or B's or C's and "talked over the last candidate for the church." He was " opposed by various people because he was too dramatic." This candidate, by the way, became an important and conspicuous minister later in life.

A collection was taken in church for the Education Society. Miss White remarks that she never will give to that object, for she doesn't propose " to help support men." Record is repeatedly made of a death on one day and the burial on the next. The names of

couples to be married are "published" on Sunday morning, and the connubial knot is tied on
the same Sunday evening.

Brief notes upon the preaching are made.
On one occasion it is recorded that Dr. Hewit
"preached rather a scolding sermon." Mr.
Hunter was famous for his sarcasm. He was
prone to hit right and left. On one particular
occasion, as he made his point in respect to
this and that and the other parishioner, a sym-
pathetic hearer in a front conspicuous pew
turned his head and nodded suggestively and
vehemently in the direction of the particular
individual who was hit by that special shaft of
wit. This gave unwonted interest and vivac-
ity to the sermon, and served to fasten the
truth permanently in the mind of the party
chiefly concerned. As an every-day and universal method of procedure, its wisdom and
charity may be questioned. But it certainly
contributed to the enjoyment and liveliness of
the town tea-parties, and helped to keep the
social life of the place from stagnation.

The second service in the parish church continued to be held in the afternoon. It was one of these afternoons, May 3, 1835, when the inn on the corner opposite the church was burned. The Sunday-school was in session. The ordinary time for afternoon meeting was two o'clock. For two hours the services were delayed, the men of the congregation lending a hand in the saving of property; but when the flames had subsided, the bell was tolled, and the people passed into the meeting-house for the usual services. While the attention may not have been close, doubtless the rest was grateful.

What a picture it makes, this long second service on a hot summer day! Here and there a head suddenly yields to its weight and topples over to one side. An occasional loud blast indicates that some one has just awakened out of a sleep and is trying to make people think he is simply blowing his nose. Several of the children have nestled down composedly by the side of parents and are gathering strength for coming frolics.

The windows are open, and the gentle cackle of ducks, with the sibilant hissing of geese, floats upon the air. Two naughty boys in the gallery have brought their fish-lines with them, and, having baited them with the refuse of the noonday lunch, they now slyly cast them forth from the windows and dangle them enticingly before the familiar fowls that domesticate themselves upon the Green. A long pull and a strong pull indicates that they have had a bite.

One boy tumbles from his seat in the excitement; the other becomes suddenly sleepy; and the poor goose sets up a cry that sets off all the fowls of the neighborhood. For a few minutes the minister's voice is drowned by the inexplicable hubbub beneath the meeting-house windows. And yet the lessons of the day are not forgotten. No sooner is the family gathered in the home, than texts are recited, the sermon discussed, the catechism taught, and the nail of truth clinched, so to speak, by the finishing touches of the home pressure.

A bundle of letters, yellow with age, gives suggestive pictures of the period. One writer speaks of the mild winter (1819). On February 7th people are ploughing the fields. Another of our good ladies writes that it is a pity the family is not in town, as they might " possibly stand a chance to push off some of the old maids" belonging to them. There are petty disturbances recorded, so we have the satisfaction of knowing that theft and iniquity are not peculiarly town characteristics to-day. There are quaint sketches of cottage routine, charitable work, village frivolity, public events. One has to use very little imagination to bring back the early days of the century, and live at second hand the life that was simple yet happy, humdrum yet fruitful, narrow yet satisfying.

A spiritual tone pervades much of the correspondence, which testifies to a reaction from the preceding skepticism. When the boys left home for business, and they were doing that sort of thing in the morning of the century here in Fairfield, the fathers and the mothers yearned over them with a fervent Christian affection. Some of these letters are fragrant with the spirit of loyalty and consecration. They show that while there was much of gayety, sport, political activity, intellectual life, in the town, there was also the grace of deep religious sentiment, the uplook and the inspiration of vital faith.

It is a fact well worth remembrance, that such a condition of things was the result not only of faithful service on the part of Fairfield ministers, but quite as much the result of fine and sterling Christian manhood on the part of laymen. People are apt to ignore or undervalue the mercies and advantages which touch them in the closest way. On the principle that no man is a hero to his valet, we are prone to think so much of what we have not got or do not find, that we neglect the things quite as precious which are distributed to us with prodigal hand.

There has always been a high tone to life here in town. The men that have won the leadership through all these centuries have been men of integrity, religious impulses, noble mind. The matters which concern both Church and State have been managed by individuals that stood for righteousness. One after another commanding personality, like Roger Ludlow, Major Nathan Gold, Captain John Burr, Governor Gold, Judge Peter Burr, General Silliman, Hon. Thaddeus Burr, Judge Jonathan Sturges, Judge Roger M. Sherman —one after another layman of such stamp has identified himself with the social, business, political, and religious life of the town to such an extent that affairs reveal a tone especially notable and praiseworthy.

Judge Sherman used to say that "either human nature was different in Fairfield than elsewhere, or that the people from the frequent exhibitions at the court-house had become disgusted with law, or that his gratuitous advice saved them from going to law ; certain it was that there was less litigation here than in any part of the country." The leading men have been Christian men, whether they were farmers, lawyers, merchants, teachers, statesmen, generals, physicians, writers, bankers, or whatever they were. It is reason for just pride and unstinted gratitude that such men have shaped the life of the town and given their manhood to its prosperity.

XI.

Judge Roger M. Sherman.

XI.

ONE is not surprised that Chauncey M. Depew, William M. Evarts, and Senator Hoar refer with keen satisfaction to their kinship with Roger M. Sherman. The sister of Judge Sherman married the Rev. Justus Mitchell, an ancestor of these famous orators.

Judge Sherman himself was the son of a minister, another illustration of the high favor granted to the offspring of this poverty-stricken class of men. In a recent letter to the writer Senator Hoar observes :

" I have sometimes thought that the present generation in Connecticut were not aware how very great a man he was. I sat a few years ago, at a Yale College commencement, be-tween President Woolsey and the Rev. Leon-

ard Bacon.   Dr. Atwater sat right opposite,
so that all three joined in the conversation.
President Woolsey told me that Roger Minot
Sherman came nearer his conception of Cicero
than any other human being he had ever heard
speak.   He said Mr. Sherman was unwilling
to speak anywhere but in court in his own
county.   He was invited frequently to deliver
addresses or orations at Yale College, but
always refused.   Dr. Atwater and Dr. Bacon
both assented very cordially to President
Woolsey's estimate of Mr. Sherman.

"When I was in Harvard Law School Professor Greenleaf, one of the most famous
lawyers and jurists of the country, told the
class one day, in a lecture, that some years
before he was journeying in the summer in his
own carriage through Connecticut.   He said
he stopped in Fairfield for dinner.   While his
horse was being fed and dinner was getting
ready, he went to the court-house, where he
found Roger Minot Sherman and Judge Gould
arguing a case on opposite sides.   He was so

interested in the argument that he remained through the afternoon, and then in the town during the entire week, for the purpose of hearing these two gentlemen's legal discussions, although he had intended to remain but an hour or two.

"I also heard a story of an eminent New York lawyer from whose clients a vessel, with a valuable cargo, had been seized on a replevin process. They thought they had a clear title, and their lawyer visited the lawyer in Connecticut, under whose direction the suit had been brought, expecting to get an easy and favorable settlement. The Connecticut lawyer really had no case. He had taken the opinion of Roger Minot Sherman, who had so advised. But he took the document and wrote on the outside of it ' Roger Minot Sherman's Opinion,' and put it on his table where the New York lawyer could see it. The name caught the eye of the New York lawyer, who thought his antagonist had got Sherman's opinion and was acting upon it. He was very much frightened, and supposed Sherman had given an opinion favorable to his antagonist, and settled the suit on good terms for the other side."

When Judge Sherman began the practice of law in Fairfield, the town still held its own among the centres of activity in Connecticut, and yet it was rather by moral force, for the trend of population was in other directions. The quiet of the place and the intellectual atmosphere were especially attractive to the young practitioner. It mattered little to him that business sought larger fields and better opportunities.

"He was a profound metaphysician," says the historian, "a scholar equal to the younger Adams, who seemed more fitly than any other man to represent the lawgiver, Roger Ludlow, and to inhabit the town which he had planted." It is interesting to note that these two men, Ludlow and Sherman, have had as much or more to do with the making of laws for this Commonwealth than any other two men connected with our history.

Mr. Sherman was not long established in his practice ere he gave himself to the various public interests of the town. He never sought office. He often declined honors. But when it was made evident that the people wished him to serve in any particular capacity, and he felt that it was within his power to serve, he manifested a conscientious willingness. Moderator of a town meeting, road commissioner, trustee of the academy, member of the assembly, deacon in the church, delegate to the Hartford convention, judge of the Superior Court—it mattered not where he was placed. He was faithful to his charge, and he contributed the wealth of his rectitude and wisdom to the problems given him to solve.

A rapid survey of his correspondence reveals the breadth of his culture and influence. Governor John Cotton Smith, Chauncey Goodrich, Senator Hillhouse, Mr. Crawford (Secretary of the Treasury), Sir Robert Peel, B. F. Butler, President Dwight, Governor Seward, Charles O'Conor, and scores of men prominent in

literature, science, law, religion, politics, education, statesmanship, were accustomed to take
counsel with him on matters of state, national,
and international importance.

In 1823 a young man by the name of Ells-
worth wrote to Judge Sherman for advice
upon the choice of a profession. Young Ells-
worth was a man of fine character and good
promise. He was a lawyer, but the ministry
seemed to present the larger opportunities for
usefulness. Judge Sherman replied : " You
have devoted very successfully a valuable part
of life to the attainment of requisite qualifica-
tions for distinction and usefulness at the bar,
and if you persevere will soon arrive, with the
blessing of Providence, to highest rank in
the profession. . . . You ought to follow the
dictates of your own heart ; your inclination
should be your rule of duty ; you will be most
useful in the employment with which you are
most delighted."

It is pleasant to remember that Mr. Ells-
worth continued to shine with the light of

Christian manhood in the legal profession, and that he became famous as professor of law, member of Congress, governor of Connecticut, and justice of the Supreme Court of the United States.

In connection with this letter is another upon the choice between the ministry and the law. In reply to inquiries, Judge Sherman observes: " All pious men in the profession of law not only may, but many actually do, accomplish much for the interests of religion and their country. In these respects I have no reason to believe that their usefulness is undervalued by the Christian community. But whatever sincerity and zeal any of them may profess, their means are comparatively limited. Without the ministry, piety would languish and ultimately expire ; the liberties of our country not long survive. Jurists are necessary to the administration of a good government ; but the preaching of the gospel is essential to its existence."

Letters of this sort were sent not infrequently to all parts of the land. Now he writes to Mr. Crawford, Secretary of the Treasury, in reference to the United States Bank.

In 1837 he writes to another Secretary of the Treasury, Mr. Levi Woodbury, on " The Enormous Expansion of the Currency beyond Natural Limits."

Again, in 1841 and 1842, Judge Sherman writes to set forth a " Plan for the Safe-keeping and Disbursement of the Public Revenue, for a Uniform Currency, and for facilitating Exchanges in the United States." This correspondence was placed in the hands of the chairman of the Finance Committee, both in the Senate and the House; and it was made the basis for plans which these committees reported to the two branches of Congress.

It is interesting to note that at one time a nomination to the position of representative in Congress was urged upon Judge Sherman, but he declined. At a later date the opportunity came when the State would have been glad to choose him to represent her in the

United States Senate; but certain views which Judge Sherman held were not agreeable to his party, and he was not willing to compromise his position.

It is evident that such a man must exert a large and commanding influence in a community. The lustre of his name was shared by the town which made his home. Gideon Welles once remarked that in his opinion Judge Sherman had but one peer as a lawyer in New England, and that man was Daniel Webster. Judge Osborne, who represented this district in the House for four years, said that he had found but one man the superior of Judge Sherman, and that was the one already named, Mr. Webster.

New York, Boston, the South, the West, sent invitations to Judge Sherman, desiring him to address them upon literary, ethical, and political questions; but he chose to tarry at home, devoting himself to the narrow round of agreeable tasks peculiar to his station and opportunity in Fairfield and Connecticut.

His devotion to local interests was unremitting. The stamp of his personality was put upon church life and social life. He conserved and fostered that type of character which is the consummate flower of the noblest Puritan traditions and influences.

It would scarcely seem fitting to speak of the contributions made by Judge Sherman to the life of Fairfield, and omit to say something about the hospitable mansion which he built and made his home. The amplitude and conspicuousness of it were unconsciously symbolic of the great man living within its walls. At the time the house was constructed it was said to be the most elegant and imposing residence in this section.

Tradition says that when the parlor carpets ordered abroad arrived in Fairfield, it was discovered they were some seven feet too long for the rooms; so it was decided to build an extension at the end of each parlor, lengthening out the rooms to the required size. It is not for the writer to assert the truth of this

tradition ; but certain it is that the wings were added, and the rooms assumed the elongated character described.   At various periods there were alterations—a piazza here and there, an extension, an additional cellar, so that there were finally three, and other improvements.

The number of closets increased until the time when the property was given into the keeping of the Congregational church.   At that period the closets numbered sixty.   They were upstairs and downstairs, in the attic and in the cellars, out of the living-rooms and out of the chambers—closets in closets, and closets in closets in closets.

That generous and noble woman, Mrs. Sherman, daughter of Judge Gould, of Litchfield, was an invalid during the latter years of her life, so she was not able to go into the second story of the mansion.   Nevertheless we are told that she kept exact account of all the contents carefully stored in this numerous family of closets ; and it was her sweet delight to dispense linen, preserves, flannels, calico, herbs,

pickles, cotton cloth, hams, and other like commodities, treasured in separate closets, to a
numerous and appreciative constituency of
friends or dependents. The beneficence of
Mrs. Sherman was limited only by the size and
number of her closets. That she was a woman
of remarkable mind is evidenced by the fact
that she carried in memory this whole laby-
rinth of closet mystery.

Her successors in the mansion have set the
limit of closets at forty or thereabouts; but
admiration of Mrs. Sherman increases year by
year, as memory fails to keep account of two-
thirds the number she arranged.

When on occasion the parsonage children
disappear for hours, and an unnatural, mysterious silence pervades that realm, and it is
at length discovered that the children are
simply lost, as it were, in the home territory
of some far distant and not recently explored
closet; or when on some other occasion the
parsonage dog is conspicuous by his absence,
and the neighborhood is explored by anxious

friends, and his departure widely advertised,
and on the second or third day the search
party call to mind that they forgot to investigate closet number thirty-seven, and after a
hasty and thorough inspection of the same
the modest animal is found quietly sleeping in
a most agreeable retirement from the trouble-
some world ; or when a new dress has been
secreted with such discriminating sagacity that
the person who secretes it loses all traces of
journey to the place of security, forgets all
about the dress itself, and some two years
later, in a fit of interesting research, comes
suddenly upon the garment, only to find that
the children have all outgrown it, and it must
now be kept for the grandchildren or sent
down to the Fresh Air Home ; when experi-
ences of the kind just noted occur, and recur,
and concur, the tribute to Mrs. Sherman's
genius is only matched by the frank expressions of shame and contempt which the present successors of the saintly Lady Bountiful
heap upon themselves.

There are worse things than having forty or
sixty closets in a house. The having none at
all, for instance. So the minister submits with
grace, cultivating a spirit of levity, in so far as
that is possible, when a dog, a child, a book, a
suit of clothes, a piece of jewelry, a pot of jam,
next Sunday's sermon, or some other piece of
property goes into strict retirement for a week,
or a year. There is a settled conviction that
sooner or later somebody will come across
the missing article. One has a feeling that
he has the thing in his possession, and that
it is perfectly safe; but just at the moment,
through some mental aberration or aggravated
imbecility, he is not able to put his hands
upon it.

But the goodness of Judge Sherman and
his wife is not to be measured by this hospitable mansion. Their good-will was expressed
by the gift of a farm.

Doubtless they saw, as it were, in a bright
vision, the light-hearted minister of the parish
rising with the birds on a May morning and

hastening forth into the fields with all the
ardor of youth. Was it grass, wheat, potatoes,
or onions that the theological tiller of the soil
sought with such enthusiasm? It mattered
not, so long as the faithful minister set his
people a notable example of early hours, enjoyed delectable intimacy with nature, and
revelled in the profits of enormous crops.

What did it concern him as to salary or no
salary? Did he not have the farm to fall back
upon, and would not this large income from
the fruit of the ground enable him to keep his
carriage or take an occasional trip to Europe?
Little did these generous people, with all their
forethought and imagination, conceive the
worth of this precious estate to their successors.

Let one throw aside all consideration of
the immense pecuniary benefit, and dwell upon
accompanying advantages. Is not the amplitude of the domain like a subtle influence
upon the personality of the minister? Room
for growth; perpetual encouragement to ex-

14

pansion, through this affiliation with broad
acres.

And what an opportunity for children?
Field upon field in which to ramble, fence
upon fence to demolish, infinite variety of
weeds to classify and become familiar with, a
skating park in the winter, a safe pond where
they can all get speedily and satisfactorily
soaked in the springtime, baseball grounds
through the summer, and always a retired and
sacred place where the whole family can wan-
der on Sunday afternoons and hide the mischief, racket, and general desolation which
appertain to that particular period on the
calendar.

Think also of the farm as a means of discipline. It is a Lord's Day morning, and the
minister has just donned his best go-to-meeting
coat, when the cry is raised that the calf has
escaped into the garden, and the mother cow
is exercising her lungs and her heels to the full
extent of the law in her chase after the wandering and frisky offspring. The minister pro-

ceeds to join the general disturbance; and just as the last bell rings, the worshippers in this land of steady habits gaze in amazement upon the whole parsonage contingent, headed by the minister himself, engaged in what appears to be a wild game of tag or fox-and-geese.   A discipline in patience!

Consider the self-control which such circumstances develop. The children of the community take happy possession of the fields, leave the bars down and the gates open, and the domestic animals vote to take a walk and a run through town by way of relaxation and variety. The news is hastily conveyed to the student buried in his books. This is a business which requires haste : so without change of garments he starts in pursuit, sending some seven or ten interested and excited helpers in as many directions in order to gather up the wandering animals. Just in the heat, dust, confusion, of the swift and successful capture of the strayed stock, some of the city brethren drive down the street, and, meeting the caval-

cade, look with amazement if not alarm upon
the hardly distinguishable features of the minister, as he seeks to avoid their gaze, and then
hears the remark, made with something of sly
wit and cunning reproach in it, " I wonder if
the pastor of the old church is going into the
cattle business ? "

Patience, self-control, fellow-feeling.   For
when the minister farms it, he watches the
skies in time of drought, and most earnestly
desires rain ; and when the season is wet, he
most earnestly desires dry weather.   When
frost and hail and blight and wind come, he
goes among the people with the same worn
and helpless expression of countenance.

But it is needless to dwell upon the matter
further.   The noble judge and his gracious
lady did a fine thing in bequeathing all these
properties and possibilities to the minister.
When we look upon the two beautiful por-
traits which adorn the east parlor of the old
mansion, and catch something of inspiration
from the two notable faces which look down

upon us ; when we gaze dreamily upon the old
clock which fills the corner of the west parlor,
and think upon the history which it has seen
made, and the famous people it has watched in
social fellowship with the master of the house
—well, it all quickens gratitude, and works to
personal enrichment.   We rejoice in the memories which cluster about Sherman parsonage.

It was when the judge was gone that the
court-house and jail were removed to Bridgeport.   The struggle was a characteristic one
while it waged.   The daughter settlement had
outstripped the mother colony in respect to
numbers and enterprise.   Business centred in
the neighboring city; and Bridgeport said
that she must have the county buildings.
Hon. John Gould headed the opposition, and
he with other citizens worked faithfully in
behalf of Fairfield; but it proved a losing battle.   The old town lost one of its most interesting features when the courts convened no
more in the little hall on the Green.   It came
like a break with the past.   And this enforced

gift to Bridgeport was to be followed by gifts
of territory and men, until it might almost
appear that the old town herself had reached
over to the city and quietly taken possession
in the name of an honored and illustrious past.

The first jail or prison in town was built in
1679. This building was set on fire by a prisoner, and burned to the ground. A second
one was soon erected. Destroyed by the British, this jail was replaced by another structure.
The last one was constructed of brick in 1853,
or partly constructed. For it was at this date
that the county buildings were removed to
Bridgeport, and the old jail property was
transformed a little later into an edifice devoted to more worshipful purposes.

XII.

Historic Memories and Rural Inspirations.

XII.

THE life of this old New England town has
had an indefinable charm. The present generation still reads Miss Mitford's "Our Village"
with delight. And while Fairfield boasted a
culture surpassed not a whit by neighboring
cities, she still retained that simplicity and
freedom of spirit which it is so difficult to preserve amid the exacting demands of great
business and social centres.

Nature had dealt generously with the village,
and people prized her friendship. To be sure,
it was Nature unadorned, for the days had not
come when men spent much time upon well-
trimmed lawns and landscape-gardening. But
even in this respect Fairfield was ahead of her

neighbors. It may not have been expedient for Mr. Hunter to speak with such wit and sarcasm concerning old fences, brier-grown yards, neglected burial grounds, slipshod houses, but the people early manifested a spirit of community pride and service.

When Mr. Jonathan Sturges laid out the grounds of his place, a landscape-gardener was employed, and the first work of the kind done in this section of the country became an object lesson of incalculable value to the State. The same spirit which prompted Dr. Samuel Osgood, later in the century, to devote many happy hours to giving Nature a chance to do her best and shine her untrammelled beauty into the eyes of men, that same spirit manifested itself on occasion during the early days. But the venerable trees, the old-fashioned flower-gardens, the open Green, the many singing birds, the changeful sea, the beautiful hills that protected portions of the town, the well-tilled acres, and the broad pasture lands where lazy herds of cattle quietly grazed or

flocks of sheep were shepherded by the boys—
these things gave an air of comfort, inspiration,
enjoyment, infinitely suggestive and restful.

Family life was sweet and eventful. Did
Tom, Dick, or Harry desire to push further into the world than farming or the law
gave them opportunity, they had simply to go
out to the suburbs of Fairfield, and business
opened before them with promise.

There was Southport, scarcely a stone's
throw from Fairfield, a thriving, lively little
borough. The regard of the mother village
for her offspring was so deep that she gave
Trinity Church to the new borough. Fearing
that one ecclesiastical organization might not
be able to cope with the powers of darkness
and the inherent tendencies to evil of the
neighbors by Pequot swamp, the mother
church again contributed a part of her life
to form another body of the Congregational
order, and a blessing was pronounced upon the
missionary task.

Another suburb of Fairfield that afforded a

fine chance for a young man was the lively
and ambitious city of Bridgeport. When the
people on the borders wanted to form a church
and support a minister, in 1695, our town was
opposed to it. The people were loath to part
with these good neighbors. But better counsel prevailed, and the first church of Strathfield,
or Bridgeport, was formed. When it came to
a desire for more territory, during this century,
Fairfield was well disposed toward this particular suburb. A generous portion of land
was handed over to the enterprising young
city. With such gift the growth and activity
of the place seemed quickened in correspond-
ing measure. So our youth were enabled to
turn their minds to trade and manufacture
with ease if they so elected.

When any son of these old and respected
families yearned for richer pastures and dreamed
of grander scenes, he had simply to push a
little farther in a suburban direction and he
came to New York. So it occurred that time
after time, when the home, the academy, nature,

and society here in Fairfield had done their
best to equip the boy, he would go down to
the great metropolis, fling himself with enthusiasm into the work, and make a fortune and a
name that rendered him conspicuous in the land.
Then came the glad return to the place of nativity, a fresh courtship of health, beauty, and
peace by seaside and in familiar fields or forests.

It was a beautiful tribute which the poet,
William Cullen Bryant, paid to Mr. Jonathan
Sturges, one of these boys that pushed for
larger opportunities. The occasion was the
retirement of this honored citizen from active
business. "I shall not offend, I hope, the
modesty of our friend," observed Mr. Bryant,
" if I congratulate his friends here assembled
that he has closed a long and prosperous
course of business without yielding to its
temptations and with a perfectly unsullied
character." It is such contributions that the
country is all the time making to our cities.
Brooklyn honors the distinguished lawyer,
Benjamin D. Silliman, with a public dinner,

and she speaks gratefully of her indebtedness to the old New England town.

When these men return to the place of nativity it becomes their joy and pride to put into tangible forms the deep affection which sweetens life. An institution like the Pequot Library, founded by honored philanthropists, named to commemorate the conflict with the Indians in 1637, is a precious fruitage of this noble spirit called local patriotism. Several of the public roads which thread their way along our levels or run back into our hills witness to the same generous and loyal spirit ; while such a structure as our vine-clad sixth sanctuary, with its setting of restful verdure and its company of stately tree sentinels, is a most beautiful memorial to the good, the true, the learned, the eminent, of the past, reared by the reverent devotion of many sons and daughters who treasure the inspirations which are fountained in by-gone generations.

Through these years there has been such intimacy between the old town and the grow-

ing centres of business, education, professional activity, that never a sign of stagnation appears. It was not an uninteresting and monotonous life which the people lived during these later days.

The tea-party still continued a popular and useful mode of entertainment. Who could make the most kinds of the best cake, was a question that required perpetual readjustment. The flavor of chipped beef and the quality of preserves were matters frequently discussed. But these things were incidental. People met for the afternoon that they might canvass the diverse and multifarious interests of the community and the nation. Newspapers were not the every-day thing that they now are. Conversation still supplied the place of periodicals to a large extent.

Then there came the weekly " sewing societies " for the ladies, and the occasional " bees " for the men. When a building was to be raised, it was considered a community affair. It is a fact that often the assembled citizens did more than raise the building ; that is to say, we have it recorded that on many an occasion they " raised Cain " as well. For these good people were nothing if not hospitable on such days. Happy thing was it for the town, if no more than one leg was broken, or rib crushed, or head smashed, by a fall from some dizzy height. And there was the annual wood-cutting, with a sort of donation for the minister, when everybody brought something or nothing, and tried hard not to carry away from the festivity more than he had brought to it.

There was also the singing school. It would be an unpardonable omission, and a notably incomplete picture of the times, did one forget these occasions when music and courtship mingled in varying proportions and furnished unlimited food for gossip, conjecture, anticipation. These were the good old times. A large proportion of the young people had voices; and the unlucky ones that did not have voices knew some one that did, so that it was necessary for the second class to be on hand that they might look after the first.

Music appeals to the emotional nature. Is it a wonder that tragedy and comedy found places in these little neighborhood gatherings? All the arts and artifices peculiar to the two sexes during the mating period of life were manifest in their manifold variations on these eventful occasions. What was said or what was left unsaid, what one did and what another didn't do, how such an one looked and how another one acted—well, it is the familiar story that is told time out of mind by people in the same interesting condition. For it is true, as Emerson says, that "all mankind love a lover." The larger freedom of these gatherings made them happily convenient for those significant and delicious love passes which were not congenial to the parlor, when the parents and small children were close at hand to note each tell-tale look, word, act.

We are also to bear in mind that Fairfield contained the usual number of interesting people. It is not necessary for a New Englander to have any nasal dialect, and illiterate way of modifying or eliding consonants and vowels, in order to be stamped as queer. People of cultivation, social standing, wealth, influence, have their peculiarities. So that life here yielded its harvest of characteristic men and women. Many are the memories and anecdotes of these people. Humor and pathos, pride and humility, sorrow and joy, sunshine and shower, they all appear in these personal narratives. A very rich treasure of character sketches might be gathered.

The academy gave its impulse to society. Books multiplied in the pleasant homes of the people. There were lectures upon the various questions of the day. Ministers like Dr. Humphrey, who became president of Amherst College; Dr. Hewit, who was promoted from Fairfield to Boston ; Dr. Atwater, who served the Prime Ancient Society here nineteen years and then went to Princeton College as professor of mental and moral philosophy—ministers like these gathered about them kindred spirits and communicated intellectual as well as moral vitality.

And there were many eminent visitors from all parts of the country who continued to make Fairfield a kind of Mecca for occasional pilgrimages. If people could not live here all the year, there were those that counted themselves happy when it was permitted them to live here a part of the year. Good men and true women, who found life's demands such that they were not able to live here any part of the year, turned with infinite loyalty and affection toward Fairfield during the last days on earth, and were glad to die here or be buried beneath its precious sod. Unto how many people did the rarely beautiful old town come to be like an earthly paradise!

The great busy world might sweep onward along the ways of traffic, conflict, ambition. But there was one old New England town begemmed with all the adornments of affluent nature. To the witchery of changeful skies, and the endless variations of form and color in landscape, there were added the many moods of the seasons, as they shifted from sad to gay, from passion of April to fretfulness of November, from a February thaw to a perfect June day, from the riot of a March tempest to the glory of an October sunset. There were the broad streets guarded by the stately lines of ancient elms and maples, their graceful branches reaching across to each other and getting lovingly entwined, so that the blue of the sky and the sheen of the sun were only occasionally seen through the vivid. green of the living archway. There were pleasant homes framed by generous yards, reposing amid a luxury of manifold trees. There were the songful birds, freely contributing their gayety and inspiration to the scene, now one company lingering a few days or a few weeks, and then another company coming on to take their places. There was the sea, averse to monotony, now blue, now green, now silver, now gold, flashing back into the eyes at eventide all the glory of rainbows, at one hour sweetly tranquil, at another hour wildly riotous, alternately fondling and abusing those who trusted themselves to her, the subdued melancholy of quiet days shading off into the strong, solemn, majestic symphony of the tempest.

Amid these scenes there seemed to tarry a throng of honored men and women. Their work, sacrifice, character, had all been wrought into the fame of the place. Their virtues continued to diffuse benedictions. Their spirit still gave tone to life and rendered sacred the ancient place. Historic memories, rural inspirations, patriotic impulses, blended into pure white light, making this old New England town a bright, particular star in the firmament of the State.

Such contribution to the good of men and the glory of this Republic has been made by one fair, quiet village of the Pilgrim and the Puritan. The work achieved by this particular town is a type of the work done by other New England villages. The current of vital influences pressing through the stream of time from old Fairfield is like to many another current of vital influences whose fountain is Plymouth, Litchfield, Concord, Lenox. These venerable and famous centres of life have taken an important part in the shaping of individual and national destiny. It is for the true American to foster this unique phase of life.

Larger and larger are the demands which the city makes upon the country. May the old New England town continue its generous gifts to the commercial, intellectual, and spiritual development of our beloved land. May the men who were born in these sequestered, beautiful places return with loyalty to the familiar associations, and write their gratitude in the tangible form of rural improvements and praiseworthy institutions.

www.ingramcontent.com/pod-product-compliance
Lightning Source LLC
Chambersburg PA
CBHW021048030726
47496CB00006B/1734